A Pekin Dewlap

THE
PROBLEM AT
WISTERIA
GARDENS

Pamela McCord

FROM THE TINY ACORN...
GROWS THE MIGHTY OAK

The Problem at Wisteria Gardens

First Edition
Copyright © 2020 Pamela Mc Cord

Acorn editor: Shelly Stinchcomb

Jacket design by Dane at eBook Launch

Book interior formatted by Debra Cranfield Kennedy

www.acornpublishingllc.com

Library of Congress Control Number: 2020918567

ISBN-13: 978-1-952112-29-4 (hardcover)
ISBN-13: 978-1-952112-28-7 (paperback)

This book is dedicated to my sisters Sheila and Michelle.

I appreciate your time and energy and love.

It makes me happy.

CHAPTER ONE

"DID YOU SEE THAT?" Pekin Dewlap asked her boyfriend. She was looking past him over his shoulder.

"See what?" Scout asked, glancing behind him.

Pekin took a moment to answer. "Nothing, I guess." She continued looking down the front walk leading from the sidewalk to her house, and Scout turned to follow her gaze.

"There's nothing there now. What did you think you saw?"

Pekin's sheepish expression gave away her embarrassment. "Well, you know when we were doing the séance?"

Scout had tried hard not to think about the Firefly Lane séance and the worry he'd felt when Pekin was prepared to let another ghost inside her head. Even though his worries hadn't been realized, he couldn't forget his anxiety. A little more than a month ago, he still had been barely able to think about anything but the first time a ghost had taken over his girlfriend's mind at Elmwood Manor and how close he'd come to losing her forever. After that disturbing event, he'd wondered whether he and Pekin and the others would ever be the same and was amazed they'd all bounced back so well.

He looked down at Pekin's face, brushed a strand of her long blond hair away from her eyes, and muttered a response. "Hard to forget."

"I thought I saw something, a gray blur, but it was only there for a moment. Maybe it was nothing."

"There was a lot going on at the time," Scout answered. "So I suppose that's possible. But is that what you thought you saw just now?"

Pekin held his gaze. "Yeah. It kinda looked like a gray blur."

"Maybe you should get your eyes checked," Scout said, winking at her.

"Very funny, Scout. My eyes are fine. But we know *this* is real." She waved the five one-hundred-dollar bills she and Scout had just discovered on her front porch, then stuffed them back into the plastic bag.

"Can I see that?" he asked.

Pekin handed him the plastic Ziploc bag, which contained the cash, a key, and a sticky note reading "Deposit," signed by someone named Matt Cooley. Scout shook it upside down to see if they'd missed anything. Nope. Nothing else was in the bag.

"Do you know who Matt Cooley is?" he asked.

"Never heard of him."

"Maybe it's for your parents," he said.

"Could be, except it had my name on the front. It might be someone who wants to hire the Ghosties."

"Too bad he didn't leave a business card," Scout said. "Or at least contact information of some kind. What are we supposed to do, stick the $500 in a drawer and wait to see if he tries to contact us again?"

"Don't tell Amber about it, or she'll want to go shopping," Pekin said with a laugh.

"Well, we have to——" Scout started to protest.

"Just kidding. Of course we have to tell her." She grinned. "I can just imagine how happy she's going to be."

Amber was one third of The Ghost Company, a business started by Pekin right before the beginning of summer vacation, and also one of Pekin's best friends, the other being Scout. So far, they'd successfully banished ghosts from two houses in Springdale.

It looked like they might have a third opportunity to help a ghost cross over.

That was a lot of ghostbusting for one summer.

Scout hugged Pekin and said good night. She watched him walk to his car, then unlocked the front door of her house and stepped inside. Hearing voices from the kitchen, she set her bag down in the hallway and headed in to join them.

She didn't mention the odd package to her parents. She didn't want to worry them, and she was also afraid they'd tell her to turn down the case. If, indeed, it was a case.

"DOESN'T IT SEEM LIKE WE spend a huge amount of time eating?" Pekin asked as the three friends slid into a booth in their favorite hangout. It had a fifties feel, with Formica countertops and red-and-white-checked plastic tablecloths. There was a jukebox in the corner, but, sadly, it was usually silent.

"This place is like our clubhouse," Scout said. "They all know us here. It's kinda cool when a soda magically appears on the table almost as soon as we sit down."

"I like that too," Amber said. "This place is so *us*."

"Yeah, and if we keep coming they're gonna charge us rent," Pekin said as a soda suddenly appeared in front of her. She flashed a big smile at the server in appreciation.

"Hey, we're growing teenagers," Scout pointed out. "We need food."

"We're lucky we can afford to come here so often. But we should be careful or all our Ghosties money will be spent on burgers," Pekin said.

Over their burgers at Benny's, Pekin and Scout filled Amber in on the odd package left on Pekin's front porch. Amber was actually excited by the cryptic message and the possibility of a new case.

"That's so cool!" Amber beamed. "I was worried we wouldn't have any more customers."

"Scout was hoping for a break, but it is kind of exciting. And very mysterious," Pekin said.

"I wonder how long it will take for him to contact us again," Amber said. "I'm really curious about what he wants us to do."

"Me too," Pekin said.

Amber dipped a French fry in ketchup. "Violet called me, by the way." Violet was the daughter of a ghost they'd recently helped cross over. Her mother, Lily, had died in childbirth and spent many years wandering through her house on Firefly Lane, sobbing over the child she thought was missing. It had been a rewarding reunion, with Violet getting the chance to meet the mother she'd never known and say goodbye.

"Really? What did she want?" Pekin asked.

"Just to thank us again for helping her mother move on. She said she was still in shock from the whole episode."

"It is kind of shocking to witness a real live ghost," Scout piped in. He held up a hand to ward off Pekin's expected practical comment that ghosts aren't alive. "Don't be Captain Obvious," he said, giving her the side eye.

"You don't know that's what I was going to say," she said, her eyebrows scrunched in a scowl.

"Okay. What then?"

It took a moment before she sheepishly confessed. "That *was* what I was going to say."

Amber choked on her French fry and gulped water before laughing out loud. "Oh, you guys."

"Sorry," Scout said, grinning widely. "I couldn't help myself."

AS THEY WERE WALKING out of Benny's, Pekin's phone rang.

"Is it Matt?" Amber asked.

"I don't know. I don't recognize the number."

Pekin answered the call. "You've reached The Ghost Company. We help you by helping them. This is Pekin Dewlap. How may I help you?"

She mouthed *I'm so professional* at her friends as she hit the speaker key.

"Hello," a tentative voice said. "My name is Sandra Martin"

"Yes, Mrs. Martin. What can we do for you?"

"I think my house is haunted. I wondered if you could, you know, help me?"

"We would be happy to assist. Can you tell me what's happening?"

"I'm new in the area. My husband and I just bought a nice older home on Tarhaven Drive. It's a lovely old place, and I really like it, but we hear strange sounds, and day before yesterday the house shook, and a glass flew off the kitchen counter. Could you come by and check it out?"

"I suppose, but we can't do it today. Maybe tomorrow afternoon?"

"Oh, that would be wonderful. I'm usually very brave, but I've been home alone while Stan, my husband, is on a business trip, and I'm a little freaked out."

"Text me your address and we'll plan on seeing you around two tomorrow afternoon. Does that work for you?"

Wrapping up the call, Pekin looked at her friends to see if they were on board with it.

"Wow," Amber said. "First we have *no* customers and now we might have two."

"Makes life interesting," Scout offered.

AFTER LUNCH, SCOUT suggested driving out to Lake Brawley and spending the afternoon on beach towels.

Amber and Pekin eagerly approved. Both were already in cutoffs and tank tops, and Scout was wearing board shorts and flip flops, so they hopped in Scout's Corolla for the half-hour drive, only stopping to pick up Scout's cooler, which they filled with snacks and bottles of water for later.

Lake Brawley was a sea of people and dogs. Boat docks peppered the west end of the lake, and the east end was a haven for RV vacationers. The area the teens settled in featured picnic tables and a wide strip of grass leading to the shoreline.

It was an uncharacteristically mild afternoon for late July. Of course, mild in Springdale still meant mid-80s, but the humidity was light. In other words, perfect weather for sprawling in the sunshine with their beach blankets spread on the grass facing the lake.

"This feels amazing," Pekin said, leaning back on her elbows on the large cotton blanket and raising her face toward the sun. Eyes closed, she sighed deeply. "We haven't done this nearly enough all summer."

"We have been kinda busy," Amber said. "Isn't it weird how none of us are freaked out that we spent almost our entire summer working instead of having fun?"

"We really need some time that doesn't have any ghosts in it," Scout said. "Let's enjoy this while we can."

"Yeah," Pekin said, worried that Scout wasn't happy about taking on a new client. "Are you sorry I told Sandra Martin we'd help her?"

"No. I guess not. Maybe it will be an easy job," he said.

"And we've been able to make some money this summer,

more than we'd have made working at a drive-thru or a normal summer job." Amber paused to take off her flip-flops. "I wonder when we'll hear from Matt Cooley."

"I wouldn't mind if he waited a week," Scout said. "And, Pekie, I don't care what job he has for us, I want you to promise me that you won't host a ghost." He looked at her sharply. "Ever again."

Hosting a ghost was a term the Ghosties made up to explain what happened when spirit entities entered people and communicated through them. Their first experience with it had been terrifying when an evil ghost took over Pekin's body. She'd been lucky that the episode had such a good ending. It was what brought Pekin and Scout together, so at least there was a silver lining. The second hosting was fairly voluntary, although Pekin expected to be the vessel, but the ghost jumped into Amber instead.

Scout was still rattled by what had happened to Pekin, and he expressed his objections often.

"Scout, you know I'm not going to promise that." Pekin frowned. "Sometimes it just has to be done." She sharpened her glare. "And I don't want you to keep bugging me about it. I promise to be careful. Really."

He shrugged. "Okay. Whatever." He turned away from her and gazed at the lake.

Pekin and Amber exchanged glances, and Amber tilted her head toward Scout, silently begging her friend to make everything right. Pekin scrunched up her shoulders and shook her head in frustration but scooted over by Scout and put a hand on his arm.

"I'll be *extra* careful if we ever face that kind of situation again. We'll make sure Mildew is there, just in case." The kids viewed Mildew, a medium who had helped when they were in trouble on their first two jobs, as a safety net.

"Scout?" she asked when he didn't respond. "Don't be mad at me."

He let out a long sigh and looked at her for a moment. Then he squeezed her hand. "I just worry about losing you," he said.

"We take care of each other," Amber said, flopping down on the other side of Scout. "Come on. Lighten up. Let's have some fun."

"Okay, then," he said, pulling a football out of his backpack. He pretended to toss a long pass. "Come on, you guys. Let's get a little exercise."

Pekin immediately jumped up and looked expectantly at Amber, who turned on her stomach and shook her head.

"You're the one who wanted us to have fun. What's the deal?" Pekin said.

"I just had my nails done Sunday. I can't take the chance of ruining my manicure."

"You're such a diva," Pekin said with a laugh, then trailed after Scout.

He tossed the ball just past Pekin so that she had to run and jump to catch it. She turned around with a huge grin, holding the ball in the air.

"You're pretty proud of yourself," Scout called, laughing as Pekin spiked the ball.

"You know it!" she responded.

Before she could throw the ball back to Scout, Amber shouted, "Your phone's ringing!"

"Who is it?" Pekin called.

"It doesn't say."

Pekin made a quick pass to Scout, then trotted back to the blanket, taking her phone out of Amber's outstretched hand.

"You've reached The Ghost Company. We help you by helping them. This is Pekin Dewlap. How may I help you?"

A man's voice responded. "Ms. Dewlap?"

"That's me."

"I'm Matt Cooley."

Pekin covered the phone and mouthed "Matt Cooley" at Amber and waved for Scout, then hit the speaker button.

"Yes, Mr. Cooley. We got your package. What—"

"You probably thought it was strange. Sorry about that. I was worried that you'd get all booked up because of being in the papers and all. I wanted to get my bid in fast." His words ran together in his hurry to get his point across.

Pekin laughed. "I assure you our phones aren't exactly ringing off the hook. But, still, what is it you want?"

"I have a situation I'd like to talk to you about. Are you available to meet?"

"I assume you're having a problem with—"

"A ghost. Yeah. And it's driving me nuts. How soon can you get started?"

"Give me a minute," she said, hitting the mute button. Looking at the expectant faces around her, she said, "What do you think?"

"He's kind of anxious," Scout said.

"Maybe pushy," Pekin noted.

"I say, let's go talk to the guy," Scout said.

"Yeah. Me too," Amber said.

Pekin clicked off the mute button. "Sure. Are you local? Do you want to meet us at Benny's around five? Do you know where that is?"

"I know where Benny's is. Doesn't everyone?" He snapped impatiently. "Five works for me."

"See you there."

Pekin lowered the phone and looked at her friends, her eyes big. "Business seems to be booming."

CHAPTER TWO

PEKIN HAD STARTED A JOURNAL after their first case at 12 Elmwood. She'd felt the need to examine her feelings following her harrowing kidnapping at the hands of George Trent's ghost. The trauma had thrown her into a cycle of dread and fear she'd never experienced before. Nightmares haunted her sleep for the first couple of weeks after Scout saved her. Writing them down helped her to sort through her thoughts and feelings and gradually let go of the horrifying crimes George Trent had shown her in the basement at Elmwood Manor. Putting down on paper what she'd gone through was an attempt to understand that experience, and it allowed her to move forward out of the cloud of anxiety that had followed her after that day.

Their next case, on Firefly Lane, featured a sad ghost who was looking for her missing baby. Actually, the baby wasn't missing. It had grown up. Lily, the mother, died in childbirth and was trapped in a cycle of searching and searching. It had been a relief that Lily wasn't scary like the evil George Trent. Reuniting the ghost with her grown-up daughter had been a happy experience, and it had helped with Pekin's fading, but still-present, anxiety.

Yes, writing helped. After the first flurry of getting down all her thoughts over Elmwood Manor, she'd found she looked forward to leaning up against her headboard, knees bent, with her serious, gray-covered journal and reviewing her day.

THE GHOSTIES GOT TO BENNY'S early to make sure to snag a private booth in the back where they could talk with their potential new client. All of them were excited and apprehensive, especially given the little package of money he'd left on Pekin's front porch.

Surprised to see them again so soon, their server had a side eye for them, disguised by a smile, and Pekin felt the need to explain that, "No, we don't eat every meal at Benny's."

Amber clutched her hands in her lap, her shoulders hunched. Scout silently sipped his soda, and Pekin's gaze flew back and forth as she watched the restaurant's front door for the arrival of Mr. Cooley. With no idea what he looked like, they watched the incoming faces for an inkling of which one was looking for the Ghosties.

A middle-aged, nervous man entered and scanned Benny's, his eyes meeting Pekin's in recognition, and hurried toward their booth, straightening his tie and tugging at the bottom of his jacket.

He stood for a moment and said, "Hello, hello," before slipping onto the seat next to Scout, and held out a hand as he said, "I'm Matt Cooley."

"Pleased to meet you," Pekin said, taking his hand. "I'm Pekin Dewlap, and this is Amber, and you're sitting next to Scout."

After introductions were over, Matt Cooley said, "So, let's get started." He signaled the server and ordered coffee and pie.

Scout cleared his throat. "Why don't you tell us what we can help you with, Mr. Cooley."

"Of course, of course," Matt said. "My shop is haunted." His gaze shifted among the teens, as if to make sure they understood the seriousness of the situation.

He shifted in his seat. "It's driving me nuts."

"Mr. Cooley," Scout said. "Can you start at the beginning, so we can catch up?"

"Sure. Sorry. And call me Matt. It's just that I want this taken care of quickly. My business is suffering."

"Have you seen the ghost?" Amber asked.

"No. I mean, I've seen the results of its infestation. You know, shelves toppled over, pictures dropped off the walls. That sort of thing."

"Do you have any idea——" Pekin started.

"Who the ghost is? Not a clue."

Scout sighed in exasperation. "We need some details, Mr. Cooley . . . I mean, Matt. How long has it been going on? When does it usually happen? Where? What kind of store do you have?"

"Okay, sure. It's been about a year, I guess. It can happen any time. I own an antique store. I inherited it from my mother, who passed away a few years back. She never mentioned anything about unusual goings-on at the shop. Anyway, that's what the key is to. You know, the one in the package I left you? Anyway, at first, I thought I was imagining things or something. The first time, I was behind the counter, which is at the front of the store, and I heard a crash from the back. There was only one customer in the store at the time, and I went to check out what had happened. I saw a Chinese Ming vase . . . probably not real Ming . . . in pieces on the floor. Weird, huh? Anyway, I hustled back up front and told the customer an old piece of china must have fallen off a shelf and broken. The customer said maybe you have a ghost and I laughed and said not that I know of."

"Could it have—" Scout said.

"It's not like we had an earthquake or something to make it fall off. I'm careful with fragile items that they don't sit too close to the edge of the table or shelf or whatever they're on. So there was no reason it should have fallen like that."

"I take it that wasn't the only thing that happened?" Pekin said.

"Nope. I'd come in some mornings and have to sweep up glass or re-shelve books that were scattered on the floor. And there was the time Mrs. Chester, a repeat customer, came rushing from the back of the store screaming that she'd seen a ghost as she burst through the front door of the store. Last time she's been in my shop. Too bad, because I could always count on her dropping a few hundred bucks per visit." He shrugged. "Oh, well. Can't cry over spilt milk, can we? And there were some other times my customers said they thought they heard footsteps behind them but when they turned around no one was there. You get the picture." He looked at the three faces hanging on his every word. "So, when can you start?"

"Tomorrow afternoon?" Scout offered.

"Sure. One, two?"

"That won't work," Pekin said. "To start, I mean. I'm afraid we have another client appointment tomorrow." She glanced at Amber, then Scout. "But we can come check out the situation on Friday if you want. Let's shoot for two."

Cooley frowned. "You can't start until Friday?"

"That's only the day after tomorrow. I'm sorry, but, as I said, we have another client we're meeting with. I'm not sure what the deal with that is going to be, so I don't know how long it will take. But you can still show us around. Would that work?"

Tightening his lips, he shook his head in irritation. "If that's the best you can do." He dug into a worn leather wallet and pulled out a somewhat dog-eared business card. "Here's the address."

"But, we——" Pekin started.

"Gotta go. Great talking to you all. See you Friday." The words were barely out before he was up and gone.

Chapter Three

~~~~~~

S COUT PICKED UP PEKIN and Amber the next afternoon to check out the potential ghost at Mrs. Martin's house.

"I've always liked this neighborhood," Pekin said as they drove down Tarhaven Drive. "All of the trees, and everyone has flowers all over. It's so pretty."

"So is her house," Amber said. "Look."

The Victorian house was white with green trim around the windows and the eaves, and the door was a deep green as well. A path bordered by pansies and perennials led up to a wide front porch.

The Ghosties pasted on smiles as Pekin clanked the brass bumblebee door knocker.

Within a few moments, a petite, dark-haired woman answered and smiled hopefully at the trio on her front porch.

"Mrs. Martin? I'm Pekin, and that's Scout and Amber. May we come in?"

"Of course," she said, then grabbed Pekin's hand and practically dragged her inside.

"Oh!" Pekin exclaimed, shuffling to get her balance.

"Sorry," Mrs. Martin said. "I'm just anxious to get started. And please call me Sandy."

"So," Scout said. "What can you tell us about the problem?"

"I have sodas, if you'd like," Sandy said. "Or would you prefer water?"

"Thanks, but we're good," Pekin replied. "We can't wait to hear what's going on here."

"When did it all start?" Scout asked.

"Beginning of the week, I think. We just moved in two weeks ago and spent the first week unpacking and putting things away, and then Stan, my husband, left for a business trip. He's a medical sales rep and has to travel a lot."

"Did he see what was happening?" Amber asked.

"I'm not sure. At first, what with moving boxes and unpacking, it's possible things were going on and we just didn't notice. But he didn't mention anything to me." She pushed a strand of hair that had escaped her scrunchied ponytail behind her ear. "It first happened right after he left on Monday. I was in bed reading when the house began to shake. I thought it might be an earthquake. I'm not sure if this area is prone to them or not. Anyway, I waited a few minutes, and it didn't happen again. When I looked around the house, nothing seemed out of place. By the next morning, I'd forgotten all about it."

She smiled nervously. "Then, that afternoon, it happened again. I heard a crash and ran to the kitchen and found a glass on the floor, smashed to pieces, and the house was rumbling around me. And there was a clacking sound. I can't really describe it."

"Is that all?" Pekin asked, beginning to have an idea of what was happening.

"No. I think I heard sounds from the attic. Like someone . . . or something . . . moving around up there."

"Maybe we should take a look," Scout said, nodding toward the stairs.

"Um . . . sure," Sandy said, and took a hesitant step toward the hallway.

When they reached the landing, Pekin suddenly said, "Oh. I forgot," and dashed down the stairs, leaving three questioning faces watching her go.

Rejoining them, she held up an object about the size of a standard flashlight. "I forgot to tell you guys. I ordered us an EMF reader."

"What's an EMF reader?" Sandy asked.

"It detects electromagnetic radiation. Ghosts are full of it. This should let us know if there's anything here that shouldn't be."

"Cool," Amber said. "Do you know how to use it?"

"It's easy. It lights up when spirits are present." She handed Scout the instructions. "All the ghost shows use this one."

"Let me see that," he said. He turned the device over in his hand and opened the battery compartment. "Batteries included." He pulled out a small plastic strip that protected the batteries until the unit was ready to be used and handed the reader back to Pekin.

She examined it. "I think you just push the button and then see if the color changes. Red means there's a ghost present." She pushed the button, but the monitor stayed on blue.

"The attic is this way," Sandy said, pointing up the staircase that ended in a door.

Amber shuddered. "That reminds me of the attic at Elmwood Manor," she said, tucking her head down in her shoulders.

"Was it scary?" Sandy asked.

"At first, it was just a huge mess," Pekin said.

"Yeah," Amber added. "A hundred years' worth of dust bunnies. We had to wash the windows because it was so dark in the house."

"The attic wasn't that bad," Scout said. "But Amber thought it was creepy. A dress dummy in the corner freaked her out."

"I don't have any dress dummies," Sandy was quick to point out.

Pekin laughed, but it was hollow sound.

They needn't have worried. When Sandy flipped on the light, it was surprisingly bright in the attic, and boxes were stacked neatly along the walls. The window on the wall opposite the door was clean, and sunlight beamed through it.

"I don't see anything out of place," Scout said.

"But I *heard* something up here," Sandy said, clutching a tissue and dabbing at her nose.

"Pekin, maybe we should give the EMF reader a try," Scout said.

She turned the unit on and aimed it around the room,

then walked slowly through the whole area. "Nothing," she said. "The color hasn't changed."

"But——" Sandy started.

"Let us take a closer look," Scout said, and motioned Pekin and Amber to join him as he looked behind boxes and up at the eaves.

"Everything's so clean up here," Amber said admiringly.

Sandy's face brightened up. "I don't like the idea of a scary attic, so I cleaned it up really well."

"Did you notice there's a little chunk missing from the window frame?" Scout asked, examining the small crevasse. He stooped closer. "And look here." He pointed at the sill, and Sandy and his friends were soon at his side to see what he'd found.

"I think those may be little footprints," he said. "Little creatures could squeeze in there. That may be what you heard. Mice or something scurrying around."

"Mice?" Sandy looked horrified.

"That happens in old attics sometimes," Scout said. "Especially in the Midwest." He scanned the area along the wall below the window. Behind a stack of boxes, he found a few strands of shredded paper, which he pointed out. "I think that's the culprit. You might want to have someone come fix that hole so nothing else gets in. I really don't think you have to worry about ghosts in your attic."

Sandy's shoulders slumped in disappointment that they hadn't found anything. With a heavy sigh, she turned, and the kids followed her downstairs.

"I'm not sure that it's just mice," Sandy said.

"Well," Scout said, "besides the fact that we found signs of mice or some other little creature, the EMF detector didn't show anything either."

"Maybe it's not working right," she said, spreading her hands in a questioning gesture.

"I read a lot of the reviews for this unit before I bought it," Pekin said. "Supposedly it will go off around a microwave. Because of the radiation it gives off when it's running. Want to test it?"

"Okay," Sandy said, and led the kids into the kitchen.

Pekin turned the unit on, and it didn't reflect anything. "Can you microwave something?" she asked.

Sandy glanced around and settled on a piece of bread. She set it on a napkin and turned the microwave on.

Immediately the EMF reader flashed the red lights. Pekin glanced at the group and held up the EMF reader. "Looks like it's working."

"But what about the shaking and the glass breaking?" Sandy asked anxiously.

"I don't know what might have caused that," Pekin said. "Let's check to see if there's any spirit activity down here." She turned on the reader and walked room to room, but, once the microwave had stopped, the meter indicated nothing else in any of the rooms.

"I'm sorry——" Pekin started to say, but a rumble, followed by shaking and a clacking sound interrupted her. "Whoa," she said, glancing around as dishes rattled on the sideboard in the dining room.

"See!" Sandy said.

A smiled spread across Scout's face. "Did you know you live a block away from train tracks?"

"What does that—" Just then, the train's whistle blew. Sandy turned bright red. "A train. It's a train that's causing the shaking. I'm not sure I'm thrilled about that."

"You get used to it," Amber said. "There are tracks close to my house too. We don't even notice it anymore."

"Oh my God. I'm so sorry. I called you out here for nothing. I feel so stupid." Her face reflected her extreme embarrassment.

"Don't worry about it at all," Pekin said. "I'm just glad we could figure out what was happening."

"I guess," Sandy said. "What do I owe you?"

"Nothing. You don't owe us anything. It was really nice to meet you, so don't feel bad about it at all." Pekin smiled and held her hands up to punctuate that everything was good.

"You can call us again if anything else strange happens," Amber said sympathetically. "We won't mind at all."

The kids waved goodbye as they climbed into Scout's car. Pekin sank back into the passenger seat and heaved a sigh of relief.

"Is it okay if I say I'm glad it turned out to be nothing?" Amber said from the backseat.

"I second that," Scout said. "Now we just have Matt Cooley to worry about."

ON FRIDAY, SCOUT STOPPED HIS Corolla in the small parking lot of Wisteria Gardens. The business card featured a homey scene with dolls and a rocking horse sitting in a corner among baskets of crocheted runners and doilies, all in a nice off-white tone.

Not for the first time, Amber said, "This card sure doesn't look like Matt Cooley. I mean, the picture on the front is so sweet and welcoming. And Matt's just . . . not."

"He said it was his mother's shop. I bet she's the one who designed the card."

"Well, I can't wait to see the inside. I *love* antiques," Amber said. "If I can stop staring at how gorgeous the outside is."

The shop was housed in a converted schoolhouse that must have dated back to the late 1800s. The shop's namesake held court outside. A breathtaking lavender-blue wisteria tree dripping with blossoms was impossible not to admire, the ground around it littered with a purple carpet of fallen petals. The wide porch in front featured pots of colorful geraniums and hydrangeas, and tall snapdragons and stocks and rosebushes were planted along the sides of the shop. A pair of cast-iron Great Danes stood sentry on opposite sides of the front door, and wrought-iron benches rounded out the welcoming exterior. The shop stood just at the edge of the downtown area, marking the border between the business district and a residential neighborhood in Carter's Hill, a small township adjacent to Springdale.

Amber made a beeline for the Great Danes, oohing and aahing as she took multiple selfies with the statues.

"Oh, I want them so much," she said. "Do you think—"

"They're probably not for sale. Besides, they look so perfect here," Pekin said.

"And can you even imagine how much they would cost?" Scout added.

Amber patted the head of the dog closer to her, her mouth turning down in comical disappointment.

The kids were intentionally early. Matt wasn't expected for another half hour. They wanted to get an idea of what they might be dealing with and then have Matt fill in any blanks.

"Let's go see if we can find the ghost," Pekin said, peeking in the door's glass window before unlocking the shop's front door. A tinkling sound greeted them when they stepped inside, and Pekin looked up to see a delicate silver bell hanging over the door.

They immediately encountered a long glass-topped counter at the front of the shop, and two aisles led toward the back. Lining the way was a surprisingly tidy array of furniture and display cases.

A laptop computer sat on the counter, and behind the counter were cupboards with sliding doors for storing business supplies. On one end of the counter, positioned on a carved wooden easel, sat a small framed watercolor of the storefront. The painting prominently featured the spreading wisteria in glorious lavender tones, with the afternoon sunlight shining through its branches causing the tree to glow.

Pekin pointed to the painting. "Whoever painted this did a great job."

"Yeah," Scout said. "It really captures the quaint charm of the place."

"Quaint charm?" Pekin said. "Did you just say 'quaint charm?'"

He laughed. "Hey, I can appreciate charm when I see it."

"He said in his most charming voice," Pekin teased.

"It doesn't smell awful in here," Amber noted. "I've been in some pretty dusty, musty shops. Matt sure does a good job with this place."

"He does," Pekin agreed. "He doesn't seem like the type, does he?"

"He's got a lot of nervous energy," Scout said. "Maybe he channels it into cleaning and organizing."

"Let's have a look around," Pekin said, and started off down one of the aisles leading through the shop. It was quiet and still inside as three pairs of eyes scanned the interior for movement of any kind.

Amber grabbed Pekin's arm. "OMG, you guys. Can you imagine if we broke something in here? We'd have to work here for years to pay it off. Be *super* careful."

They exchanged wide-eyed looks and continued their tour of the shop.

Other passages connected the two aisles, enabling customers to meander through the shop. In the back was another long display case, featuring a hodgepodge of farm implements like iron hooks and milk jugs, not to mention rusty pulleys and glass doorknobs and a wooden butter mold.

"Look at this," Amber said, picking up a pretty porcelain doll. "I always loved these."

"Amber!" Pekin glared at her friend. "Put that down before something happens to it."

"Geez. I was being careful. Besides, how much could this cost anyway?" She flipped over the price tag. "Eek! It's six-hundred dollars!"

"Step away from the doll, Amber," Scout said in his most intimidating voice, causing both girls to bend over, giggling. Amber gingerly set the doll back on the counter where she'd found it. Far back on the counter.

Also in the back was a supply area next to a backdoor and a small kitchenette with a water cooler, coffee maker, and an old refrigerator. Amber opened the refrigerator door to find bottles of water and not much else, other than a carton of half-and-half.

"I guess he's not much of a snacker," she pointed out. Next, she examined the supply room and pointed out a bag of cat food. "But he must have a cat that is. I can't wait to meet it."

Shelves of dishes and knickknacks lined the walls, jockeying for position among faded paintings and old sepia-toned framed photographs, and dressers and tables supported bygone dolls and stacks of books, with trays of jewelry inside glass-topped display cases scattered throughout the shop. Scout admired an old player piano, which occupied its own carved-out space. He lifted the cover and thoughtfully ran his fingers across the yellowing ivory keys.

"My grandfather had one of these," he said. "It was spooky to watch it playing with no one touching the keys." A box of piano rolls sat to the side of the aged piano.

"Were you scared of it?" Amber asked, grinning wickedly.

"Maybe when I was three, but I got over it," he said, and smirked back at her.

Pekin stopped to inspect wooden racks draped with timeworn, discolored linens and quilts. There was a musty smell coming from them, something that would be impossible to dispel without laundering the ancient, fragile items. Her foot caught at the edge of an aging Persian carpet, faded and threadbare, and she windmilled her arms to keep her balance. "That was close," she said, putting a hand over her face in mock horror.

The kids wandered the aisles and carefully sat on the red velvet Victorian sofa, not sure whether it would collapse under their weight. Photographs and portraits of long-dead ancestors of people who also might have passed on, and mirrors whose glass was streaked by age, hung in a surprising grid-like formation. More than a few dressers, tables, and bedframes hulked here and there. A box with toys spilling from the top peeked out from under an oak table. An old black Underwood typewriter with stick on letters in black and gold, spelling out PAM, graced a solid oak gate-leg table whose wings were folded, most likely to conserve space. Perhaps it had once been someone's prized possession. There must have been hundreds of items covering every spare inch of the shop.

But no ghost.

They explored the outside grounds of the property, peeking through the windows of an old shed behind the shop, and wandered through the crowded furniture aisles for another twenty minutes.

But no ghost.

Even Pekin's EMF reader, which she'd flashed around the shop as they explored, didn't blink red to indicate any otherworldly presence.

"What should we do?" Amber asked, looking wilted after prowling through acres of forgotten treasures.

"Matt should be here anytime now," Pekin said. "We'll get the whole story from him. I'm just sorry we couldn't find the ghost before he gets here."

"Me too," Amber said, frowning with disappointment. "At least we tried."

"He should be able to wait a few days. We don't have to work all weekend."

The tinkle of the bell over the door sounded, and the kids trouped toward the front of the store.

Matt greeted them with a forced grin.

"Is everything all right?" Pekin asked. "You don't look—"

"It's fine. Just in a hurry to get this all over and done with."

"We understand. This weekend doesn't work for us, so we'll start first thing on Monday. I'm sorry. I hope you understand."

He waved them off. "We'll deal. So, what happens now?"

"We're hoping you can give us some clues or something," Scout said. "Maybe, if you tell us how it all started, we'll be able to figure out the direction to take."

"There are some sofas around," Pekin said. "Should we all go sit down?"

Matt led them to a small grouping with the red Victorian sofa and chairs they'd noticed earlier, and they all took a seat.

"Can you start at the beginning?" Scout asked.

"Hmmm." Matt's eyebrows scrunched together as he tried to recall anything that might be of help.

"Tell us about the shop," Amber offered.

"Oh, well, as I mentioned to you before, it was my mother's. She passed away five years ago."

"We're sorry to hear that," Amber said.

He waved her off. "I'm over it."

"Still—"

"Let's get on with it, shall we?" Matt squirmed a bit and leaned forward, resting his elbows on his knees, his hands clasped. "Mother died five years ago. She owned this place for a good twenty years before she passed away. Of course, as her only living heir, I got the shop. I had my own real estate business but found myself enjoying being at the shop. I guess I felt close to Mom here. I decided after a while to take a break from my company and see what I thought of running an antique store. Turns out, I like the slower pace. Real estate can be hectic; everyone's in a hurry. Rude clients and paperwork up to your eyeballs. And I felt like I was always behind. Then I come to this little shop, and it's peaceful. I don't have to deal with hours spent troubleshooting for clients, rushing to meet their never-ending deadlines."

"Were you and your mother close?" Amber couldn't help asking.

"Yeah. I loved my mom. Like everybody does."

"Being her only son, she must have doted on you," Amber continued.

He sighed. "She did, now that you mention it. I think I took it for granted. But we spent a lot of time together. I had a house down the street from her, and we had dinner together once or twice a week. And I came in here now and then to help out."

"You really keep it neat and clean," Pekin said.

"Yes, well, that was my mom's doing. She was a stickler for cleanliness, and it must have rubbed off." He stared off into space as if lost in a memory.

"I like that painting of your shop on the front counter," Pekin said.

"My mother painted it," Matt said with a warm smile.

"She was really talented."

"She was taking painting lessons when she passed away. She loved it. That was one of her best works."

Pekin smiled encouragingly. "I'm sure it's a comfort to you to have it."

Matt nodded.

"About when did you start noticing disturbances?" Scout asked, to steer the conversation back to the reason they were there.

Matt sniffed. "It was about a year ago. At first, there was some rattling, kind of like if there was an earthquake, but nothing broke. And when I looked around, I didn't see anything out of place, so I didn't think anything about it."

"Are there any train tracks around here?" Amber asked.

"No. Why would you ask that?"

"Well, a client we just met with was having problems with dishes rattling, and it turned out to be trains passing by."

"I can assure you, that is *not* the problem here," Matt said indignantly.

"Did your mom ever mention anything strange happening when she ran the shop?" Scout asked, trying to smooth Matt's ruffled feathers.

"No. No, she didn't. She would have had me check it out if she had." He scratched absently at his nose. "Anyway, I forgot about the rattling, and nothing happened for a while after that. Then, one afternoon as I worked on the books at the front counter, I heard a crash and found a painting had fallen off the wall. I turned over the painting to see what the problem might be, but the wire on the back was still attached, and the hook was still in the wall. I wondered what would make the wire jump off the hook. It didn't make any sense. Nothing else happened that day, and I eventually forgot all about it."

"Did the customers start noticing things around the same time you did?" Scout asked.

"No. I started getting complaints a couple of months ago."

"Like?" Scout asked.

Matt chuckled. "Mrs. Bartlett was hemming and hawing over an old pitcher and bowl set. She mentioned a few times that it was too pricey. She'd leave it and mosey around the store but always ended up back at the pitcher and bowl. I was at the front counter reviewing the books when I heard a crash, and Mrs. Bartlett came running up the aisle. 'The pitcher and bowl!' she howled, pointing over her shoulder. 'They flew off the dresser and broke.' She followed me back to the spot where the glass remains lay in a heap on the floor. Of course, I was certain that Mrs. Bartlett had caused it, but she claimed she'd been in the next aisle over at the time. She insisted she wasn't paying for the damage when she had nothing to do with it and left in a huff when I tried to find a rational explanation for the broken dishes."

"Seems like there could be a rational explanation," Pekin said.

"Yeah. I thought so too. But two days later another customer appeared at my elbow, her face white as a ghost, and said a pair of shoe skates had rolled down the aisle past her. She said they turned the corner. Her voice actually rose an octave when she said *they turned the corner*. So, of course, I rushed back to the spot where she said it happened. She pointed out the route the skates had taken, peeking around the armoire that marked the intersection of two aisles. I followed and peeked over her shoulder. No shoe skates. I didn't even remember having any shoe skates in the store. I apologized and offered her a ten percent discount the next time she came in. She said something about not coming back and rushed out of the shop." He paused to glance around the store. "Then there were the usual ghost things. Upended furniture, dishes flying off shelves. That kind of thing."

Pekin, who'd been making notes on her tablet, looked up. "Did it get cold in here?"

"Well, yeah. It's cold in here during the winter months. And the shop's air-conditioned, so sometimes it can feel a little chilly. I usually wear a jacket when I'm working. Looks more professional."

"No, I mean, unnaturally cold. Usually, when there's an entity present, there's a chill in the air. A really cold chill."

He paused as if considering the question. "No, I don't recall feeling really cold. Are you saying, if it isn't cold, then I don't have a ghost?"

"Nooo," Pekin said, drawing out the word. "I mean, it's been our experience that cold air can announce the presence of a ghost, but I suppose it's possible it doesn't always happen that way."

"You're sure you can't start until Monday?" Matt said, looking sharply at Pekin as if to convince her to change her mind.

"I'm sure. We're sorry, but we have some conflicts. I promise we'll jump right on it Monday morning."

He frowned. "All right. Fine. But if that changes . . ."

"We'll let you know," Pekin said.

"THANKS, PEKIE, FOR NOT giving in on the Monday thing," Scout said.

"Yeah," Amber added. "We want to enjoy our weekend. And I'm going up to the mountains with my family and won't be back until Sunday night anyway."

"I want a weekend for fun too," Pekin said. "Monday's soon enough. He waited a year. What's a couple more days?"

"What do you think about him not feeling a chill when the activities were going on?" Scout asked.

"No idea," Pekin responded. "We'll have to see for ourselves when we start the job. I personally think, if there is a ghost, it'll be cold."

Scout stopped his Corolla in front of Amber's house, and he turned as she opened the back door to get out of the car. "Have fun in the mountains. I'm kinda jealous."

She laughed, sticking her head back inside the car. "Thanks. Maybe we should plan to go sometime. It's only a two-hour drive. We'd have a great time up there. I'll miss you guys."

"Us too," Pekin said, watching Amber head up to her front door. "Have fun!" she called to her friend out the car window.

"Hey," Scout said to Pekin as he pulled away. "Wanna do a movie tomorrow?"

Pekin smiled and nodded. She still couldn't quite believe that Scout was her boyfriend now. They'd been best friends—the three of them—since grade school, but it wasn't until last year that Pekin's feelings for Scout had changed, and she'd suffered real pangs of jealousy when Vanessa Dooley, with the perfect face and long sable hair cascading down her back, flirted with him. That was before Scout saved Pekin from the evil ghost of George Trent, who had snatched her away to hide her in a secret room. Before Scout said he wanted to be *her* boyfriend.

And, now, only two months after Scout's fateful declaration, Pekin basked in the joy of having a boyfriend for the first time. Though they were taking their time getting used to their new relationship, Pekin enjoyed every minute they spent together. And Amber enjoyed teasing Pekin about being in love. Enjoyed it a little too much. Amber had a boyfriend of her own, Josh Parker, and it was obvious she felt justified in teasing her best friend mercilessly simply because Pekin and Scout's relationship was so new.

Scout dropped Pekin at her door, giving her a quick kiss before she jumped out of the car. She watched him drive away from her front porch, already thinking about the next day. She could hardly wait.

CHAPTER FOUR

RIDAY. TODAY WAS INTERESTING. We finally met Matt Cooley, the guy who left that package on my porch. I mean, we met him a couple of days ago, but today we saw him in his element. He owns an antique store. You'd think someone who owns an antique store would be old and sweet. I mean, not sweet exactly. Maybe kindly is a better word. But Matt is sooo not. He's kinda strange. So nervous! Always fussing with things, straightening something sitting on the counter or picking up a dish and putting it down again. I hope this job goes quickly before our entire summer is gone.

Pekin set aside her journal, picked up her little gray cat, and plopped down on her bed. "Life's been interesting this summer, Griselda," she said, snuggling the little feline. "And I have a date with Scout tomorrow." She closed her eyes and smiled.

PEKIN AGONIZED OVER THE perfect outfit, finally settling on her best jeans and a clingy new T-shirt she hadn't worn yet. She was admiring herself in the full-length mirror on her closet door when Scout texted he was out front. She texted back she'd be down in a minute and headed for the bathroom to add lip gloss and a little blush. She brushed her long blond hair up into a ponytail, then shook it out, then shrugged and pulled it up again into a ponytail.

Calling goodbye to her mom, Pekin grabbed a light jacket for the cold theater and her purse on the way out. She stepped onto the front porch and stopped in her tracks when she saw Vanessa Dooley standing a little too close to Scout. Vanessa was smiling up at Pekin's boyfriend, and her hand was resting on Scout's arm. Pekin cleared her throat as she approached.

"Pekin," Vanessa said dismissively, looking down her nose.

"Vanessa," Pekin responded, trying to control the glare that wanted to laser out of her eyes.

"I was just telling Scout that the cheer squad is planning a party before school starts again and told him we were asking the football players to come help us set up." She smiled up at Scout. "And inviting them, of course." She looked at Pekin with a small smirk. "And Scout's agreed to help."

"He has?" Pekin felt a stab of betrayal. "But—"

"He can tell you all about it," Vanessa purred. "I have to run. Have to get the word out. You two have a nice day." She turned and walked away, glancing back at Scout with a conspiratorial smile.

Pekin's smile was forced. Scout started around his car to the driver's side, when Pekin said, "I'm not feeling well. I think I'll just stay home tonight." She turned to walk toward her front porch.

"Pekin," Scout said. "Wait. It's not what you——"

"What I think? You don't know what I think. I'll talk to you later." She stuck her key in the door, muttering, "Maybe," over her shoulder. Inside, she leaned against the door, anger and jealousy dancing around each other in her head. Sniffling, she stomped up the stairs to her room and slammed the door, startling Griselda, who had been curled into a ball on her bed.

"Sorry, sweetie," Pekin said, sinking down beside the little gray cat and burying her face in her hands. "What am I going to do?" she wailed before curling into her own ball around Griselda.

There was a knock at her door, and her mother, Melissa, stuck her head in. "Are you okay?"

"Oh, sure. I'm getting a headache and decided I didn't feel like going out."

"Did Scout do something——"

"No, Mom. I'm fine. Really." She rolled over, her back to the door.

"If you're sure. Do you need an aspirin or anything?"

"No. I just want to be alone." She squeezed her eyes closed, trying desperately not to cry in front of her mother. She didn't need any mom advice at the moment.

"Whatever it is, honey, things will work out. You'll see."

"Mom!"

She heard the door click closed and let the tears come. So many emotions were churning in her head, foremost the fear that she'd wildly overreacted. But it was Vanessa

Dooley! And she said Scout was going to help her. And she was touching his arm.

And Scout was never going to speak to Pekin again.

Still, when Scout texted to ask what was wrong, she chose not to respond.

PEKIN WOKE UP SUNDAY MORNING with a headache and red, puffy eyes. She soaked a washcloth with cold water, wrung it out, and lay back down on her bed with the damp cloth on her eyes, hoping if she waited long enough it wouldn't be obvious that she'd cried herself to sleep.

Her mother looked at her a little too sharply when she went down to breakfast, but Pekin waved her off, saying she was feeling much better. "Can you drop me at the mall?" she asked.

She hoped a little retail therapy would help her feel better, but she suspected it wouldn't. She was at war with herself over whether she should blame Scout for going to the dark side or blame herself for showing just how insecure she really was. Where was Amber when she needed her?

Her texts to Amber weren't answered, probably because there was sketchy cell phone reception in the mountains where her best friend was spending the weekend. Knowing that didn't help, because she really wanted someone to sympathize with her.

When her phone dinged, she was sitting on a bench outside Macy's sipping a mocha. It was Scout calling. Pekin debated for a moment whether to answer, took a breath, then clicked the Talk button and said hello.

"Pekie, what's going on? What happened last night?" Scout asked, his voice reflecting his concern over Pekin's actions.

"Nothing. I told you I didn't feel well." Her stomach was churning in anxiety.

"Where are you?"

"I'm at Rosehill Mall. I had some shopping to do."

"I'll be right there."

"No, don't. I'm not sure how long I'm going to be here." She just couldn't face him. Whether it was anger or embarrassment, she didn't want to examine her feelings too closely.

"Well, can I see you later? I can come over this afternoon and we can—"

"I don't think so, Scout. Maybe tomorrow." She held her breath for a moment. "Okay?"

"Yeah, sure," he said. "I'll talk to you some other time." And he was gone.

She looked at her phone after he ended the call, unsure what she should do. She wasn't used to feeling like this. Amber would tell her what to do. But Amber wasn't available. Pekin didn't know how she'd get through the rest of the day without her best friend.

By the time her mother picked her up from the mall, she'd decided maybe she should explain herself to Scout. But he didn't call. Not that afternoon, not that night.

Pekin moped around the house, avoiding her mother's questioning gaze. She made excuses for herself, claiming that nothing was wrong and she missed Amber. She busied herself cleaning out her closet, which was so unlike her that her mother wanted to take her temperature.

Later, in her room after dinner, a tear dripped on the pages when Pekin opened her journal. She sniffled and wiped her nose.

Sunday. *I think I really messed up this time. Scout's not talking to me and I don't blame him. I was so mean to him after I saw him talking to Vanessa Dooley. He wanted to talk it out but I was too mad, and then he got mad, and now I don't know how to fix it. What if it's all over between us?*

Pekin could have cried in relief when Amber called Sunday night. In fact, at the sound of Amber's voice, Pekin burst into tears. Amber told Pekin that whatever was wrong, together they'd fix it and said she'd be right over.

Pekin sat on her bed, rocking back and forth and cradling her stomach. She was a pitiful sight. Her head flew up when she heard the doorbell. She rushed to the landing at the top of the stairs and called to her friend to come up.

"You kids want anything?" Pekin's mother asked as Amber started up the stairs.

"No, thank you, Mrs. Dewlap," Amber said, as Pekin called down a weak "No."

Amber followed Pekin into her room, pulling the door closed behind her.

"Oh my gosh, Pekie," Amber said, alarmed at her friend's red eyes. "What happened?"

"Scout hates me!"

"Scout doesn't hate you. Whatever happened, you can

count on Scout. He doesn't hate you." She grabbed Pekin into a hug, and plopped on the bed. "Tell me everything."

"I was *awful* to him," Pekin said, her eyes filling again. "I didn't go out with him on Saturday like we planned, and I didn't answer his texts. Then he stopped texting. I haven't heard anything from him in *hours*."

"Well, first, why were you awful to him?" Amber reached over and took her friend's hand.

Pekin looked down, unable to meet Amber's eyes. "Because of Vanessa Dooley."

"*What?*" Amber jumped up. "What did Vanessa do?"

Pekin didn't answer right away, and Amber said, "Unless Scout planted a big, mushy kiss on Vanessa, why are you fighting with Scout over *her?*"

Amber sat back down and picked up Pekin's hand again when she saw the miserable look on her friend's face. "Come on, Pekie. What happened?"

"Scout came to pick me up yesterday afternoon, but, when I went outside, Vanessa Dooley was there. She was doing the flirty thing and batting her eyelashes at him. And her hand was on his arm and—"

"That was all Vanessa, Pekie. Was Scout flirting back?"

Pekin pressed her lips together and shook her head. "No."

"Did he look happy talking to her?"

"No."

"Did you get mad at Scout because she was there?"

Pekin squirmed. "I guess."

"Then what?"

"Well, I told him I didn't feel well and went back in the house."

"So, Scout was ambushed by Vanessa, and you blamed him for it?"

"It sounds pretty awful when you say it like that." It was Pekin's turn to stand and pace. "I realize I wasn't being fair, but now Scout's mad at me and I don't know how to fix it."

"You march over to Scout's and apologize," Amber said. "He didn't do anything wrong."

"I know he didn't. I just freaked when I saw Vanessa. And she conned him into helping her set up a party."

"Oh, hmm," Amber said. "That's unfortunate. And he said yes?"

"She said he did. And she smiled at me all smarmy-like. I wanted to vomit."

"So, instead, you blamed Scout?"

"I did!" Pekin wailed.

"Text him right now and say you want to talk to him."

Pekin picked up her phone. "All right." She took a deep breath and started typing: *Scout, can you come over? I'm sorry I acted like a witch.*

When he didn't respond immediately, Pekin's anxiety grew with each minute that passed. Amber offered lame reasons for Scout not texting back, but her words didn't ease Pekin's worry.

Both girls jumped when Pekin's phone dinged.

I'm busy. I'll pick you and Amber up tomorrow morning to go over to Matt's. Around ten.

Pekin looked up at Amber. "See! He hates me!"

"He doesn't hate you. He probably *is* busy. Don't worry. You can talk to him tomorrow when you see him on the way to pick me up. You can fix this, Pekie. Scout adores you."

"He *did* adore me. Now he hates me." She collapsed back on her bed. "I'll never be able to sleep tonight." She threw her arm over her eyes. "But maybe you're right. *Maybe* he'll forgive me."

"Tomorrow isn't that far away. Don't fret all night. Read a book or something." Amber picked up her bag and headed toward the door. "And don't cry anymore. You don't want to have bright red eyes when he sees you."

OF COURSE, PEKIN TOSSED AND turned all night, but she made a valiant effort not to cry because . . . red eyes.

She was quiet when she came downstairs for breakfast. Her mother kept glancing her way, worry creasing her forehead. Pekin realized she needed to appear more cheerful before her mom started in with questions about what was wrong, and she pasted a smile on her face and gushed, "These look delicious," when her mother placed a stack of pancakes on the table in front of her. "Thanks, Mom."

"You're meeting your new client today?" Melissa asked.

"We already met him, Mom," Pekin said, a hint of snark in her voice.

"I *meant* you're meeting *with* your new client today."

"Yes, we are. Scout's picking me up in a little while and we're going to go check out the haunted antique store."

"Can't wait to hear all about it," her mom said, carrying her cup of coffee out of the kitchen.

Pekin didn't have much of an appetite, so she cut her pancakes up in little pieces, hoping it would make them easier to swallow. Still, she did little more than push them around on her plate. After a few forced bites, she washed the evidence down the garbage disposal and put her plate in the dishwasher.

She carried her backpack into the den to wait for Scout, thinking about the best way to make everything better.

Too nervous to sit quietly, she peeked out the front window every few minutes until she saw his Corolla pull up to the curb, then she called a "Bye" to her mom, grabbed her backpack, and went out to face her fears.

Her face fell when she saw that Amber was already in the car. It could only mean Scout didn't want to be alone with her. It pinched her heart, but she called out a cheery hello to her friends as she took her place in the front passenger seat.

There wasn't much conversation on the drive to the shop. Amber tried to lighten the mood by talking about her family's trip to the mountains, but Scout drove silently and Pekin stared out the window on her side, mumbling a response to Amber when appropriate.

In less than half an hour they arrived at their destination.

Pekin was relieved that, as they drew near to the shop, the tension evident on the drive over was replaced with anticipation and curiosity about their newest case.

CHAPTER FIVE

THEIR FIRST ACTUAL DAY on the job was a disappointment. Despite spending the morning trying everything they could think of to lure the ghost out, there were no sightings. The kids spent their time wandering among the antiques, examining any interesting things that caught their eye, and staring at each other. Amber found her way out the front door to continue her admiration of the two Great Danes guarding the shop.

Pekin watched Scout whenever she thought he wasn't looking. He was still quiet, only responding when she asked him a question. She felt like a cloud of gloom was hovering over her, but she did her best to appear optimistic and cheerful. It didn't help, however, when Amber shot her sympathetic glances. Pekin worried Scout might notice.

After a couple of unproductive hours, Pekin was ready to throw in the towel anyway.

"I don't think Matt's going to be happy with us," she said. "But what else can we do?"

"Maybe there's not really a ghost here?" Amber offered.

"Then how can you explain all the broken dishes and odd

occurrences Matt and his customers experienced?" Pekin asked, frustrated at their lack of success in discovering what was going on in the shop.

"I don't *really* think there isn't a ghost," Amber said. "I can't explain anything."

"I can't believe I forgot my EMF reader at home," Pekin said. "Maybe we could have found the ghost with it. I'll stick it in my backpack tonight so we have it tomorrow."

"Should we bring some candles or something, just in case? Mildew always comes prepared."

Pekin sighed. "Have we learned *nothing* from Mildew? I'm sorry, you guys. Why didn't I think of those things?"

"It's okay, Pekie," Amber said. "We just started this job. We'll be more prepared tomorrow."

"I guess we can call it a day, even if it's only noon. It seems like Matt's ghostly visitor has taken the day off," Pekin said, feeling dejected.

"Who's hungry?" Seemingly feeling relief at ending their surveillance of the shop for the day, Scout rubbed his hands together as he waited for the expected affirmative responses from his friends.

"Want to check out places to eat in Carter's Hill, or should we just go to Benny's?" Pekin asked.

"I want to go home," Amber grumbled.

"You're not hungry?" Pekin asked, surprised.

"I'm starving. I meant Benny's. We can check out Carter's Hill another time. We'll be back here tomorrow anyway."

"Hopefully we'll have more luck then," Pekin said. "I'll

check with Matt tonight to see if there was any ghostly activity after we left."

"It works out well for us that he only has the shop open in the afternoon. That gives us plenty of time to devote to finding what's haunting the place before he comes in." Scout unlocked his Corolla, and the three kids piled in for the twenty-minute drive back to their home turf.

PEKIN RECEIVED A CALL FROM their client in the middle of dinner. She said she'd call him back later, and she did. Matt Cooley seemed unhappy with the lack of progress the Ghosties had made that morning. Pekin explained that, until they had a sighting, there wasn't much they could do to get rid of the ghost. She reminded him that they'd just gotten started. It was their first day on the job. They were just getting a lay of the land for now.

"I don't know why you couldn't see it," Matt said, his voice tight. "It was bugging me this afternoon."

"We'll try again tomorrow," she said. "Hopefully—"

"Well, call me before you're done. I want to know if you see the ghost."

Pekin sighed, feeling uncomfortable that their first day had been a bust, at least in Matt Cooley's eyes. "Okay. I will."

She texted Scout and Amber to tell them about her conversation with their client and her worry about their lack of progress.

We just started. It's too soon to think we're going to fail. It's not our fault if the ghost doesn't want to cooperate, Scout said.

Yeah, Amber chimed in. *I bet we'll find something tomorrow.*

Pekin wandered back into the kitchen to help her mom with the dishes after speaking with Matt and texting with her friends.

"So, no luck today?" her mom asked.

"No, and I'm a little bummed."

"Remember, Miranda didn't show herself immediately the first day you went to Elmwood Manor."

"I know, but there wasn't a hyper client breathing down our necks when we were at Elmwood. Matt is *intense*. You'll have to meet him." She glanced at her mother. "Maybe you shouldn't meet him actually. He's a real tyrant."

Melissa smiled as she squeezed out the sponge she'd used to wipe down the counter, then put a hand on Pekin's shoulder. "I forgot to tell you about Mrs. Wagner. She passed away this weekend."

"Our neighbor?"

"Yes. Poor dear. I think she had a heart attack."

"I liked her. She always bought Girl Scout cookies from me. And she had a cute cat. What happened to Sparkle?"

"I don't know, dear. It didn't come up."

"I'm sad now."

"Me, too. But she had a nice, long life, bless her heart."

"Thanks for telling me. I'll say a prayer for her."

Pekin started up to her room but turned back. "Mom, do we have any candles?"

PEKIN SAT ON HER BED FOR A minute, stewing, before

deciding to call Mildew. Pekin was nervous about their new client and was hoping for some comforting words from the little medium who'd been a lifeline to them in their first two cases.

"Have you ever had a pushy customer?" Pekin asked after the usual *how are yous.*

"Oh, yes," Mildew replied. "Not everyone is a dream to work with. Some people are uncooperative. Some are very demanding. Some are just unpleasant. What's yours doing?"

"He wants immediate results. We were over there and didn't detect anything ghostly." Pekin paused when Griselda hopped up on the bed, and she pulled the little cat onto her lap. "Oh. And guess what? I got an EMF reader. I even used it at Matt's shop . . . that's our customer . . . Matt. But it didn't do anything."

"They're helpful to have. I think you'll find it will come in handy at times."

"Matt called tonight to complain about our lack of progress in getting rid of his ghost." She threw up her hands even though Mildew couldn't see her. "But we can't get rid of it if we can't find it."

"Everything will work out, dear. Some ghosts are stubborn. Maybe if you three sit quietly and clear your minds, the ghost might get curious and want to see what you're up to. Just a thought. I think you'll figure out what to do, but, if I can help in any way, be sure to give me a call."

"Thanks, Mildew," Pekin said. She ended the call and tossed her phone on the bed, then buried her face in Griselda's soft fur.

"You never complain about me," she murmured as the little cat purred.

THE NEXT MORNING, AS THEY DROVE TO MATT'S, THERE WAS a feeling of anticipation and worry about whether they'd see any sign of the ghost. Climbing out of the car, the kids looked uneasily at the antique shop, feeling a pressure they hadn't faced on their first two jobs. Matt Cooley was a whole different animal.

"He reminds me of a lion impatiently pacing back and forth in its cage," Amber said. "We're doing the best we can after all."

"It would sure be helpful if we had some idea who the ghost might be," Pekin said. "Then we could address it by name. Maybe that would make it want to show itself."

"I know," Amber said. "I don't think we can tempt this ghost out by reading *Harry Potter* to it."

"Yeah. Miranda was an easy ghost in comparison," Pekin responded.

"You're right," Amber said. "Miranda was special. I miss her. Maybe we should get her to hang out with us while we wait for this ghost to show up."

"Since we don't know what kind of ghost *this* one is," Pekin said, "maybe we should hold off on that." She smiled warmly at Amber. "But nice thought."

"Let's get this show on the road," Scout said, pushing off from where he'd been leaning against the side of his car. "Think positive."

Pekin's hand shook as she unlocked the shop's front door, not from fear of what might await them inside, but from concern that they would fail at their task.

Scout gave her a comforting grin. "Don't worry, Pekie. We got this."

She relaxed, so happy to have her friends, her boyfriend especially . . . if he *was* still her boyfriend . . . at her side as she pushed open the door.

The three kids stood inside waiting to feel something . . . anything . . . that would indicate they weren't alone. But it was warm in the shop, and silent. Pekin sighed as she flipped on the light switch.

"This is going to work," she said, more to encourage herself than her friends.

She rummaged in her backpack for the EMF reader and stuck it in her back pocket, giving a heavy sigh of frustration.

The shop wasn't large enough that they needed to split up to cover more ground, so Scout and Amber followed Pekin down the aisle to the right of the display case. Her voice wavered a little as she called out, "Anybody here?"

No answer. She pulled out her EMF reader and turned it on. She pointed it in several directions, but no red light appeared, so she turned it off and stuck it back in her pocket.

After the first walk-through, the kids parted to continue their quest to contact whatever spirit haunted the shop.

"Ewww!" Amber's voice brought her friends to see what had happened. She was shaking her foot and her face was contorted in a comical look of horror and disgust. "Ewww! Ewww! Ewww!"

"What's wrong?" Pekin asked, noting Amber's scrunched eyebrows and open mouth that screamed revulsion.

"I stepped in a bowl of water," Amber whined, pointing at the puddle on the floor. "Why is there a bowl of water? It wasn't here yesterday. And I had to step in it!"

"We'd better clean up that water before it leaves a spot on the wood floors," Scout said. "I'll see if there are paper towels in the restroom."

"Don't you care what happened to me?" Amber glared, her hands on her hips.

Scout couldn't help rolling his eyes. "You're not going to die from stepping in a bowl of water. Let's clean it up."

Amber turned pleading eyes on Pekin, obviously hoping for backup. "Pekie?"

"It must have been awful," Pekin sympathized. "Your flip-flop is all wet."

Amber shook her foot again. "I know. It's creepy."

"I'm not sure creepy is the right word," Pekin said. "Unfortunate. It was unfortunate that you stepped in it."

Amber glanced around the shop and shouted, "Why is there a bowl of water on the floor, ghost? Come out here and explain it!"

Scout arrived with the paper towels and began mopping up the puddle. "Did the ghost answer you?" he asked, looking at the floor to conceal his amusement.

"No. The ghost did not answer," Amber responded with a huff, and pointed at Scout. "I can see you trying not to laugh. Stop it. It's not funny." Then she doubled over in giggles. "JK."

Scout wadded up the sopping paper towels and handed them to Pekin while he tore another few sheets off the roll. She grabbed the soaking wet ones and ran for the restroom to minimize dripping water all the way to the trash can.

The water bowl fiasco was the most excitement they had during their ghost watch. Despite trying the EMF reader several times, there was never any indication of spirit activity in the shop. It was a disappointed trio that filed out of the antique shop and piled into Scout's Corolla.

"I don't know what to do," Pekin moaned. "Should we give Matt back his money and admit defeat?"

"We're not defeated, Pekie," Scout said. "It's only been two days, and we didn't really start until Monday. Remember, Miranda didn't show up right away either."

"I know, but Elonia wasn't jumping up and down and breathing down our necks."

"True, but don't let Matt scare you. He may be paying us, but he can't get rid of the ghost by himself. He needs us."

CHAPTER SIX

〰〰〰〰〰〰〰〰〰〰〰〰〰〰〰〰〰〰〰〰〰〰〰〰〰〰〰

NO ONE FELT UPBEAT enough to try a new restaurant, and Benny's was always welcoming, so they voted to go to Benny's for lunch. Pekin was still disappointed, her burger sitting untouched while Amber and Scout both wolfed theirs down almost as soon as the burgers were set in front of them.

"And Matt wanted me to call him when we left his shop instead of waiting for tonight." She groaned. "What am I going to tell him?"

"You're going to tell him it's only been a couple of days. Eat your burger and we'll call him after lunch," Scout said.

"Pekie, we've crossed over two ghosts. We're awesome!" Amber said. "Come on. Snap out of it. We've got this."

Pekin had to smile at that, and she did perk up, sitting straighter and taking a renewed interest in her burger. When she'd finished eating, she squared her shoulders and said, "Let's go face the dragon."

Scout laughed and smothered her in a hug. "That's the spirit, Pekie. So to speak."

Despite the hug, Pekin knew Scout was still mad at her. But she'd take any sign of affection she could get.

They filed out of the restaurant and sat down at one of the picnic tables outside Benny's. Pekin took a deep breath and punched in Matt's number. He picked up after two rings.

"Mr. Dooley . . . Matt . . . you asked me to call you after we left your shop, so I'm just checking in."

"Did you see it? Did you get rid of the ghost? I can't wait to have that thing gone."

Pekin squeezed her eyes shut before she answered. "No. Unfortunately, the ghost didn't make an appearance. We spent hours there, calling for it to come out, but nothing happened."

She heard his loud groan through the phone.

"Well, then, you'd better get back here because I'm pretty sure it's the ghost rattling dishes in the back of the store."

"Really? It's there now?" Pekin's eyes grew big, and a smile spread over her face. She looked at her friends for confirmation and then said, "We're on our way."

There was excited chatter in the car on the drive back to the antique shop. Nervous chatter. Nervous anticipation.

Matt opened the door to greet them the moment Scout's Corolla pulled up to the curb and waved energetically to hurry them inside.

"Do you hear it?" he asked, glancing around the interior.

The Ghosties exchanged concerned looks. Scout cleared his throat. "We don't hear anything. Can you still hear it?"

Matt cocked his head. "No. Not now." He leveled a stern look at each of them. "But it'll be back any minute."

Searching for something to say, Pekin settled on Amber's mishap. "There was a bowl of water on the floor in the back. Amber accidentally stepped in it, but we cleaned it up. Did the ghost put it there?"

"No, that's for Trixie. She's back there somewhere."

"Trixie?" Pekin asked.

"My mother's cat. Mother let her have the run of the place, and I usually bring her with me. For the company."

"Can we see her?" Amber asked, her eyes lighting up. "I love cats. Pekin does too. She has a cat named Griselda."

Matt harrumphed and started toward the back of the store. "Come on, then."

A sweet-looking, pleasingly plump black cat with white paws was perched lazily on one of the display cases, casually licking an extended hind leg. As her tail twitched, white could be seen at the tip of it, and, when she lifted her head to inspect the humans invading her space, the kids saw patches of white gracing her chin and the front of her chest.

"She's so pretty!" Amber exclaimed.

"She doesn't seem worried," Pekin offered. "Usually, animals freak out when spirits are around."

"Trixie used to get scared when there were occurrences of paranormal activity," Matt said, "but I think that ghost is feeding her. I've noticed cat food spilling out of one of the kibble bags I keep in the little storage area in back. I know *I* didn't spill it. And it's happened more than once. They're old buds now."

As if in agreement, Trixie lifted her head, and Pekin could have sworn there was a grin on her face.

The temperature was warm. No sudden chills settled over the room.

"Are you kids anti-ghost or something?" Matt asked with a frown. "It was making a racket up to the moment you stepped in the door."

"Matt, I assure you—" Pekin started.

He raised a hand to stop her. "You know, I didn't used to believe in ghosts. I was pretty sure there was some vandalism going on . . . that was what was causing all the ruckus. But I've been here when it happened and could never find a single person hiding in the store. The back door is always locked unless I need to go out there for some reason, and no one can get past me while I'm manning the counter up front. And you noticed the bell that rings whenever the front door opens? Well, it hasn't rung before there's ghostly activity."

As they filed up toward the front of the store, a crash caused them to turn around. Pekin expected to find Trixie near a broken plate, but she saw that the cat hadn't moved from its place on the counter. It was looking intently to the right, and a glance in that direction showed a wooden crate lying on its side on the floor, small iron toy soldiers spilled around it.

Trixie went back to grooming her other hind leg as the kids and Matt surveyed the mess. He knelt and picked up one of the toy soldiers. "My God, these were mine. I never knew what happened to them." He stood, still holding the toy. His gaze swept the area where they stood. "Where are you?" When there was no answer, his face clouded. "What's the matter with you? Are you a coward? Come out this instant!"

Pekin cringed. "Aren't you afraid to make it mad?"

"What's it gonna do, break more dishes?"

Pekin and her friends shared uneasy glances, but all three seemed to relax when several moments passed and nothing happened.

"What are you guys going to do to get on top of this ghost thing?" Matt demanded.

"We'll come back in the—"

"That hasn't been working. You have to do something else." Matt glared at Pekin until Scout stepped between them, causing Matt to tone down his rant.

"We're doing everything we can. I even brought my ghost finder," Pekin said as she pulled the EMF reader out of her back pocket. "It didn't register any ghost activity either. It's not our fault the ghost won't come out while we're around. It's possible the ghost is attached to you."

"To me?" Matt shuddered. "Well, get it *off* me." He stomped off toward the front of the shop.

The kids caught up with him by the cash register. "We could try having a séance," Pekin said. "Then, hopefully, we can make it cross over."

"You do still want us to come back tomorrow, don't you?" Scout asked.

"Yeah, sure. I just won't hold my breath."

Chapter Seven

~~~~~~

N O ONE WAS FEELING particularly optimistic when they climbed out of Scout's car the next morning and stared up at the antique shop—their nemesis.

"Let's get this over with," Amber said with a frown.

"We have to be optimistic," said the less-than-optimistic Pekin. "I feel good about today."

"Not sure why," Scout muttered, then, glancing at Pekin, added, "but I'll be optimistic, too, if you want me to be."

"I want us all to go in with a positive attitude. So far, it's all we've got," Pekin said as she unlocked the front door and pushed it open.

They didn't exactly march into the shop so much as slump through the door.

Pekin rubbed her hands together. "Okay. Let's go find that ghost." She held her EMF reader out in front of her.

As she started toward the back of the shop, the meter lit up, and a wavery figure appeared in the aisle before her, causing Pekin to stop in her tracks and Amber, and then Scout, to crash into her.

Amber opened her mouth to complain, but when she

saw the form shimmering in front of Pekin, her eyes flew open wide, and she clutched her friend's arm.

STOP! DON'T YOU DARE! the entity shouted.

"Wh-who are you?" Pekin stammered, backing into the warm huddle of her friends and shivering at the chill spreading through the air in front of her.

STAY OUT OF IT, DO YOU HEAR ME?

Pekin straightened out of the crouch she'd hunched into and plastered a determined look on her face. "We want to help you cross over," she said in a voice that sounded more controlled than she felt.

Well, I don't need your help, and I want you to butt out.

And then it was gone.

The Ghosties breathed a collective sigh of relief.

"Well, that happened," Scout said.

"Was that an old woman?" Amber asked. "I was kind of too scared to stare at it."

"Looked like it," Pekin said, recalling a plump elderly woman wearing what appeared to be a pink polyester tracksuit fitting a little too snugly. "We should try to get her back."

"How?" Amber asked. "I don't know what we did to get her to come out this time."

"She wants us to stop doing something," Scout said. "But we haven't *done* anything."

"Maybe she overheard us talking to Matt yesterday?" Amber offered.

"It's possible, I guess," Pekin said. She tapped her chin with a finger, her brows knitted together in thought. Suddenly, a huge grin spread across her face. "It was the séance. *That's* what she doesn't want us to do. She heard us tell Matt we could try that and he said to go for it. She doesn't want us to get rid of her."

"Makes sense," Scout said.

"Let's test it," Pekin said, and then said in a loud voice, "Let's plan our séance. We can have our expert medium, Mildew Willingham, help us so we can be sure to cross over the spirit."

Immediately there was a loud crash. The kids followed the sound to find a large blue vase shattered on the floor. A disembodied *Noooo* floated in the air.

Pekin put her hands on her hips and glared into the air. "If you don't want us to do a séance, you better come out and tell us why."

All three Ghosties held their breath.

The plump pink-clad ghost with over-teased orangey-red hair billowing around her head plopped into the aisle in front of them, more solid than she'd appeared the first time. *You can't do that.*

Pekin glanced at her friends then said, "I'm Pekin, and this is Scout and Amber. We're here to help you. Don't you want to be released from your earthly bonds?"

No! Butt out!

"We can't do that. We've been hired by the owner of this shop to . . . to . . . ." She looked helplessly at her friends.

Get rid of me? The ghost suddenly started to sob, and the Ghosties looked at each other in alarm.

"Well," Pekin said, "you're scaring his customers."

They're my *customers! This is* my *shop!*

"What's your name?" Pekin asked. "Tell us who you are."

The ghost glared at her. *My name is Althea. That ungrateful person who hired you is my son.*

"How's he supposed to know that?" Amber asked. "He can't see you."

You can see me, the ghost pointed out.

"We've had practice," Pekin said.

"Yeah, you're not our first ghost," Amber added.

"I think maybe your son is too, um, Type A to be able to connect with your spirit," Scout said.

Type A?

"You know. Nervous, driven, ambitious. It seems like he's moving a hundred miles an hour."

The ghost actually chuckled. *That sounds like my Mattie.*

"We've learned to make our minds quiet, so that's probably why we can see you," Amber said.

"Why don't you want to cross over?" Pekin asked.

Because I don't want to be separated from my son. I love him. I want to wait for him.

"That's a new one," Scout said under his breath.

You can't take me away from Mattie. If you try, I'll . . . I'll break every dish in this place! Althea tried to appear fierce, and she stamped her foot in dismay when the three kids giggled behind their hands.

Laugh at me at your own peril, the ghost warned.

"We don't mean to laugh, Althea," Amber said. "But you're so cute!"

Althea sputtered. *You think I'm* cute? *How dare you? And*

she waved her arms sending a chill wind howling through the shop, rattling dishes and causing more than one picture to fall off the wall. She brought her arm back like a ballplayer and swung it forward with force, and a gravy boat smashed on the floor in front of Pekin, so close that the Ghostie had to jump back.

Take that! Althea snarled.

"Unacceptable," Scout said sternly, moving to stand between Pekin and the spirit. "If you keep that up, we'll definitely have a séance and send you away." He spread his fingers in an explosive gesture and said, "Poof!"

Pekin clutched Amber's arm, her adoring gaze on her boyfriend. "Scout's protecting us. Isn't he wonderful?"

The ghost started to cry again. Big gulping sobs shook the ectoplasmic form, which was ethereal to begin with, and Althea was suddenly less solid.

"Just adorable," Amber responded, "but is she all right?"

"Well, she's *dead*," Pekin said.

"You know what I mean," Amber said with a frown.

Althea wailed louder and said, *No, I'm not all right. He tried to explode me!*

"You threw a vase at me!" Pekin responded, hands on hips. "I could have been injured."

Humph. Don't be so dramatic. Besides, it was a gravy boat, not a vase.

"*I'm* dramatic? I'm not the one throwing vases. And breaking dishes and—"

"And," Scout interjected, "why would you want to destroy your own store?"

Because, Althea said. *Because, I wanted him to notice me.* The ghost turned her back as her shoulders shook with her sobs.

"Oh, Althea," Amber said, reaching out a tentative hand toward the spirit. "I'm sorry we yelled at you."

Althea looked back over her shoulder, her sobs downgrading to sniffles. *You want to send me away.*

"Well, usually, spirits *want* to cross over. To go to heaven or wherever and want to see their loved ones who've passed before them," Pekin said. "We just want to help."

You're not helping. You're interfering. Mattie and I are just fine without your meddling.

"I'm not sure Mattie is just fine," Pekin said. "And we're not meddling. We were hired to do a job."

"We're kind of at a standstill here," Scout said. "I'm not sure what we should do."

You can butt out.

"For goodness' sake, Althea, stop being such a grumpy old woman," he said.

I'm not an old woman, the ghost said with a humph. *I'm just older.*

"And that's as old as you're going to get," Scout said.

How dare you, you rude young man.

"Oh, will you two stop sniping at each other?" Pekin said, her gaze jumping back and forth between Scout and Althea. "We need to figure this out. Any suggestions?"

"Well, I guess the first thing we need to do is tell Matt that his mom is still here," Amber said.

"And, you," she continued, addressing Althea, "you need to stop being so grumpy. No one will want you around if you're always crabby."

The ghost stopped mid rant and stared at Amber. *I'm not always crabby. I'm a very nice person.*

"We haven't seen that side of you yet," Pekin said. She studied the small group for a moment. "Why don't we start over?"

"I'm willing to if *she* is," Scout said, watching Althea.

The ghost stared at them for a moment. *This isn't what I expected it would be like.*

"What do you mean?" Pekin asked.

Well, that I could be having entire conversations with people who are still living. I mean, I've seen a lot of scary movies, and the ghost doesn't sit around chatting. It usually just rattles chains and stuff.

"Is that why you're breaking dishes? Because there aren't any chains around?" Amber asked.

No, that was only an example. I just mean, this seems so normal.

"I'm kind of surprised you have enough energy to keep talking," Scout said.

I am beginning to feel faint. Maybe I should go.

"No!" Pekin said in alarm. "We need to figure out what to do."

Well, I might start fading away, Althea said.

"Then stick around until you have to fade," Pekin said.

This is so weird, Althea said.

"Why don't you go rest up for a couple of hours?" Scout

offered. "Then you can come back, and we can talk more before Matt gets here. We don't want to tire you out."

With that, Althea disappeared.

"Why'd you tell her to go away?" Pekin asked.

"It gives us a chance to talk among ourselves and figure out what to do."

"Can we go get something to eat? Amber said. "All this haunting stuff is making me hungry."

"As if I'd say no to food," Scout said with a grin.

WITHIN MOMENTS, EVERYONE WAS loaded into Scout's Corolla, heading for Carter's Hill's main street to check out lunch options. Amber's eyes grew big when she spotted a Mexican restaurant, and she made her desire known to her friends.

"Tacos are never a bad idea," Scout agreed, and pulled into a parking space located serendipitously in front of the restaurant.

Since it was early for the lunch crowd, they had no problem getting seated in a booth right away. Chips and salsa immediately appeared as if by magic.

Scout closed his eyes in appreciation as he bit into his first salsa-dipped chip. "This was such a great idea, Amber."

Pekin looked around. "This place is cute. I like the arched doorways and piñatas. And it's cool that we can watch the tortillas being made on that round machine."

"And it's really colorful with all the pictures of desert flowers and plants," Amber added as a server approached their table.

Once the server had taken their orders, it was time for the Ghosties to talk.

"Matt's going to be surprised," Amber said.

"No kidding," Pekin said.

"It's a weird situation," Scout added. "I mean, your mom is haunting you and wants to stay. Do you *want* to send her away?"

"I don't know how I'd feel," Pekin said, "but Matt's so . . . so . . . complicated."

"Is that a nice way of saying he's difficult?" Scout kidded.

"I wouldn't say he's *difficult*," she said. "Just kind of forceful, or determined. Something like that."

"I guess our job will be to act as a mediator between the two of them," Scout said. "We have to figure out if we want to convince Matt to let her stick around or convince Althea to cross over."

"Or we just give him the facts and let him decide," Pekin said.

"Ghosts are so strange," Amber piped in. "I mean, they're all so different. Miranda was hesitant and sweet and trusting. George was a monster. Lily was sad and unapproachable until we reunited her with her daughter. Althea is a pistol. She's kind of like a teacher scolding you."

"A rude teacher," Pekin added, taking another chip and dipping it in the salsa.

"I'm kind of on Althea's side, though," Amber said. "She doesn't want to be parted from her son." She covered her mouth and giggled. "Mattie."

"I think Matt will understand," Pekin said. "We'll

explain the situation to him and ask if he's okay with her hanging around."

"Yeah," Amber said. "But what if he wants her gone? Poor Althea. She'll be heartbroken."

"I know, but Althea's not our client. Matt is."

"That's the bottom line," Scout said. "If he wants her to move on, we have to tell her. No matter how disappointed she'll be."

"We should get right back after lunch so we can talk to Althea before Matt comes in at two," Pekin said. "I wish I felt good about all this."

"Well, *I* feel good," Amber said brightly. "This case is all about love. Isn't that cool?"

"Ask me after we see how Matt feels about having a ghost for a permanent resident."

CHAPTER EIGHT

〰〰〰〰〰〰〰〰〰〰〰〰〰〰〰〰〰〰〰〰〰〰〰〰〰〰〰〰〰〰〰

"WE'RE BACK, ALTHEA," Pekin called when they stepped through the shop's front door.

Nothing.

"Althea!" Amber yelled.

Nothing.

"What's wrong with that ghost?" Amber asked. "Now what?"

"Now we get tough," Scout said. He winked at his friends and continued in a louder voice, "Let's call Mildew and get that séance scheduled for this afternoon."

Nooo! The eerie wail was followed by Althea shimmering into view. *You can't do that.*

"You won't give us much choice if you don't behave," Scout said.

You're not a very nice young man.

"And you're not a very nice ghost," he said. "But we've already established that. Now, are you ready to get down to business?"

The spirit did its best to show its irritation with the

process, crossing its arms and harrumphing. The scowl on Althea's face would have been intimidating if they didn't have the séance to hold over her head.

"We need to tell Matt that it's his mother haunting the store," Pekin said. "And," she addressed Althea, "you need to respect his wishes if he doesn't want you to stick around."

You can't make me leave. She flew into Pekin's face. Pekin, who refused to be cowed by the ghost, darted toward her and waved her arms, causing Althea to shrink back.

"Well, there's the séance thing," she said. "But, besides that, why would you want to stay where you're not welcome?"

He's my son. He loves me. Of course he'll want me to stay.

"Maybe you're right," Pekin said, "but it should still be his choice. Life is for the living, and I'm sorry to point this out, but you're not living anymore."

How can you be so cruel?

"I'm not being cruel. There's no good way to say it." Pekin drew in her breath. "So, are you onboard with abiding by your son's wishes?"

Humph.

"I'll take that as a yes." Pekin placed a finger on her chin and narrowed her eyes. "I was wondering about something, Althea. Matt took over the shop after your . . . passing, but you didn't show up until a few months ago. Why didn't you appear sooner?"

Oh, I was here. I yelled and waved my arms right in his face, but he wouldn't notice me. I can't tell you how upset that made me.

"Well, obviously he couldn't see you," Amber said. "You're a ghost."

I'm a ghost now and you can see me.

"We've already gone over that," Scout said. "But it doesn't explain what took you so long."

That's what I'm trying to tell you. When Mattie didn't pay any attention to me, I got madder and madder and, over time, I discovered, if I concentrated really hard, I could make things move. But he still didn't notice because I could only move them a little. So I practiced. And practiced. And, voilà, now you see me.

"Lucky us," Scout said under his breath.

Pekin put a hand on his arm and shot him a glare.

"Thank you, Althea," Pekin said. "We appreciate it."

"We met your cat," Amber said, grinning.

I know. Trixie. Isn't she adorable?

"Yes. I love cats. Is it true she's not afraid of you because you spill out food for her?"

I had to make friends with her after . . . you know.

"Can she see you?" Amber asked.

Oh, yes. She looks right at me and meows. It means she wants her treats.

"That's so *adorable*," Amber said. "We'll do our best to convince Matt to let you stay, okay?"

Would you? I only want to be with him until he can join me over here.

"He should be back any time now," Scout said. "And then it'll be time for the big conversation."

Should I stick around?

The bell over the front door rang before anyone could answer the ghost. "Hello," Matt said, spotting the three teens. "Any luck?"

"Yes, actually," Pekin said. "We need to talk to you."

"What's to talk about? Can you get rid of it or not?"

"It's not that simple," Scout said. "You might not want—"

"Trust me. I *want*."

"But—"

Just then the bell rang again, and three middle-aged women stepped inside. Matt called a cheery "Welcome to Wisteria Gardens," and approached the group. He immediately busied himself with asking what they were looking for and offering to answer any questions they might have. He glanced over his shoulder at the kids and said, "I don't need to know anything about it. Just come back tomorrow and get rid of it. Now, if you don't mind." He shooed them out of the shop before rejoining the ladies.

"That didn't go the way I expected," Pekin said. "He didn't give us a chance to tell him about Althea."

The three stood on the sidewalk looking back at the antique shop. "What do we do now?"

"Should we wait until the customers leave and try again?" Amber asked.

Before anyone responded, another car pulled up at the curb, and an older couple exited and approached the antique shop.

"Could be a long wait," Scout noted.

Heading toward the Corolla, Pekin said, "I guess we come back tomorrow. We should come back before Matt gets there so we can talk to Althea."

"Don't you think she heard what he said?"

"Maybe, and, if she did, she might be angry," Pekin said.

"I'm a little worried about what we'll find when we get there in the morning," Scout said, sticking his key in the ignition and starting the car. "I guess we'll find out."

CHAPTER NINE

〰〰〰〰〰〰〰〰〰〰〰〰〰〰〰〰〰〰〰〰

THREE WORRIED TEENS stood outside the shop's door the next day.

"It could have been worse," Pekin said once they were inside and she had scanned the overturned tables and broken dishes.

"Maybe it is," Scout said. "We haven't seen the rest of the store." A trail of items dumped off shelves and pictures hanging crookedly on the walls continued toward the back.

"Althea," Scout said loudly. "You've made quite a mess."

Althea shimmered into focus standing on top of one of the counters, a blue china vase in one hand.

If Mattie thinks I'm going to go quietly, he can just think again. Can you imagine? He can be so stubborn, but I'll make him regret sending me away. Just you watch!

The blue vase sailed over their heads and crashed into an oak dressing table, and the ghost's head swiveled on its neck as it looked for the next item slated for destruction.

"Calm down, Althea," Scout said, holding up a hand. "We'll talk to him today and make him understand. But you have to agree to abide by his decision. If he wants you to go, you need to go."

But I can't leave him, the ghost wailed.

"Don't you have family to greet you when you cross over?" Amber asked. "Wouldn't you like to see them?"

They've waited this long, they can hold out a little longer.

"Still," Amber continued, "if your son should decide he doesn't want you to stick around, doesn't it give you comfort to know you'll be seeing your loved ones again?"

That's a defeatist attitude. Make him let me stay.

"I can see where Matt gets his stubbornness," Scout said with a frown. "He's just as determined to evict you as you are to stay."

Humph, was the ghost's peevish response.

"Look," Pekin said, suppressing the urge to sigh in exasperation. "We'll do the best we can. You know your son. Getting through to him is difficult. But we'll see what we can do. Okay?"

Fine. I'll be watching you. And she was gone.

"She's kind of a pill," Amber said.

"She's certainly single-minded," Pekin added.

"Who's claiming her?" Amber asked.

"What do you mean?" Pekin asked.

"Well, so far, we've had three ghosts, and it sort of breaks down to one each. Pekin, you befriended Miranda first, Scout, you rescued Pekin from George Trent, and I got inhabited by Lily. But we have to be careful not to tell Althea about Miranda."

"Why not?" Pekin asked.

Amber put a hand up to shield her mouth in case the ghost was listening. "Because, Miranda decided not to leave. If Althea knows we helped one ghost stick around, she'll expect us to do the same for her."

"I hadn't thought of that," Pekin said.

What's that? a ghostly voice floated on the air. *What about other ghosts?*

"Oops," Amber said, pulling in her head and grinning sheepishly.

"You're not our first ghost, Althea," Pekin said. "So far, we've successfully solved all our cases."

Who's Miranda? I heard that short girl say not to talk about Miranda. Did you fail?

"No, we didn't fail," Pekin said, pausing to think fast. "We successfully freed Miranda's spirit from that old house she'd haunted for a hundred years."

The ghost narrowed her eyes, not sure whether to believe Pekin.

"I'm not that short," Amber said, drawing herself up to her full five foot two and scowling at Althea.

Oh, don't be so sensitive. How else can I tell you apart? The short one, the blond one, and the boy.

"Or, you could use our names. I'm Amber, that's Pekin, and the boy is Scout."

What kind of name is Pekin? That's a stupid name.

"You're unbelievably rude, you know that?" Scout said. "Let me tell you about how good we are at our job. Miranda Talbert was our first ghost. She was a fourteen-year-old girl who'd been abducted in 1918 and never found. Her spirit was trapped in an old mansion with the ghost of George Trent, the man who murdered her. George snatched Pekin and hid her in a secret room. With help from our medium friend, Mildew, we rescued Pekin, and convinced George, with some arm-twisting, that it was in his best interest to cross over. Which he did. Miranda's bones were found buried in a garden shed, so she was free to leave as well. Then we were hired to help a sad ghost named Lily. She'd died in childbirth, so she would have spent eternity looking for her baby if not for us. We found her daughter and reunited them so Lily knew her daughter was okay, and then Lily went into the light. So, don't think we don't know what we're doing."

Humph, the ghost mumbled, apparently her favorite response.

"We'll do our best," Pekin said again.

"Your son will be here shortly. Maybe you should go wherever you go so we can do our job," Amber said.

"But you should be ready to come out if we need help convincing Matt who you really are," Scout said.

Fine. Don't screw it up.

"You know, Althea," Pekin said, "your attitude might make us not really want to be on your side. We might be more sympathetic if you'd show some gratitude."

Fine, the ghost said through tight lips. *Thank you for helping me.* And she was gone.

"Why do you think she's so *there?*" Scout asked.

"*I* think it's because she has such a pushy, domineering personality," Pekin said. "It followed her after her death. She's her own energy source."

"It's like talking to a real person," Amber said with a shudder. "I kinda wish she was more ghostly."

"I know what you mean."

"We don't have any idea what her relationship with Matt was like. Were they close? Did she drive him nuts?" Scout's face turned serious, all humor gone. "Their relationship in life is probably what will cause Matt to decide whether he wants her to cross over or to haunt him while he's still here."

Pekin pulled bottles of water out of her backpack and handed one to each of her friends. "I guess we wait for Matt to show up and try to get a few words in before any customers show up."

"Or before he cuts us off. He doesn't want to hear anything except that we got rid of his ghost." Scout held up his hands in frustration. "We can't let him get away with it this time."

"Oh, you guys. I forgot to tell you," Amber said. "My mom is making me and my cousins sing a song at my grandparents' fiftieth. Some song about love and a recliner."

"What?" Scout said. "I don't know any songs about a recliner."

"I think she means 'Evergreen.' It's an easy chair, not a recliner."

"Yeah. That's it."

"How do you know that?" Scout asked.

"It's from an old movie I watched with my parents and grandparents a long time ago. My mom went around singing that song for days."

"Gaah!" Amber said. "Can you even imagine how much I *don't* want to do it?"

"Why?" Pekin said. "You have a really pretty voice. Remember you sang in that one program?"

"I was in fourth grade! I'll be so embarrassed."

"It's just your family," Pekin said. "No one's going to be judging you."

"It's my family and my grandparents' rich friends. It's at their country club. I only have two weeks to learn the song."

"I'll help you learn it. I still remember some of the words. It's such a romantic song." She started humming the tune.

"Thanks, but I think I'm going to be sick of it after singing it for two weeks."

"Well, if you need any help," Pekin said, "let me know."

Tinkle, tinkle went the front door.

"Matt's here," Scout said, heading to meet their client.

Matt set Trixie's carrier on the counter near the cash register, and the moment Matt opened its door, the little cat hopped down and disappeared into the back of the store. He turned to face the kids and rubbed his hands together, a big grin on his face. "Tell me you got rid of the ghost."

The Ghosties exchanged glances, and Pekin said, "It's not that simple."

"What's the problem?" Matt's grin disappeared, replaced by a frown. "Are you incompetent or something?"

"That's just *rude*," Amber said. "Your ghost doesn't want to leave."

"I don't care what the *ghost* wants," he sputtered. "I'm the one paying you."

"Can we back up a minute?" Scout said, pushing his palms down in a placating gesture. "Just let us tell you what's going on."

"Well, I—"

"If you'd stop interrupting us," Pekin said, "we'll tell you everything. Can you just listen?"

"Fine. Why don't you tell me why you can't get rid of the ghost haunting my store?"

"Geez," Scout said. "We didn't say we *couldn't* get rid of it."

"Then what's the holdup?" Matt said, glowering at Scout.

"It's your mother," Scout said.

"What? My mother's dead," Matt said.

"Exactly."

"Exactly what?" Matt asked. Then it was like a lightbulb went on in his head. "My mother is haunting me?"

"That's what we've been trying to tell you," Pekin said. "She doesn't want to leave you."

"Yeah," Amber said. "Because she loves you too much to be separated." She turned away from Matt. "Although I can't imagine why," she muttered under her breath.

Pekin shot her a look, and Amber made a motion of zipping her lips.

"How do you know she's my mother?"

"Because she's loud and pushy and stubborn," Pekin said. "And because she said so."

"You can't be serious," Matt said. "That's just absurd."

"What? That a mother loves her son so much she doesn't want to leave him?" Amber asked.

Matt squeezed up his shoulders and rolled his eyes while shaking his head in a shivery motion.

"I just don't know if I believe it," he finally said. "What did she say, exactly?"

A scrabbly sound startled them, and, as a group, they filed into the back of the shop, only to find Trixie happily munching on kitty kibble scattered on top of the display case.

"Did you kids leave that out?" Matt asked, scowling.

"No. We didn't," Pekin said. "It was your mom. She and Trixie are friends now."

Matt waved his hand at broken glass and crooked pictures throughout the shop. "Did you kids do this?"

Pekin sighed loudly. "Oh my God! Why would you think *we* did it when it was happening long before you hired us? It was your *mother*. She heard you last night when you said to get rid of the ghost. You didn't give us a chance to tell you it was her. She was mad, so she carved a path of destruction through your store."

He shook his head again and turned toward the front. "This is too much. I just want that ghost gone."

A shriek sounded through the store, followed by a loud *NO!*

Matt whirled back around, eyes wide in surprise. "What was that?"

"That was your mother," Pekin said, thinking *how dense*

is *this guy?* "Look. We can prove it to you. Think up a question that only she would know, and we'll ask her."

"That's silly," he responded.

"You're impossible," Amber said, glaring at Matt. "You want to know what it is, but, when we try to tell you, you refuse to listen. Why don't you just sit down somewhere and let us tell you what we know?"

"I didn't sign up for this," he muttered.

"Actually," Pekin said. "You did. And we have the deposit to prove it."

Outnumbered, Matt led them back to the cozy seating area with the red velvet Victorian sofa. It also sported three high-backed Queen Anne chairs arranged around an old steamer trunk covered by a crocheted runner and decorated with a dainty china tea set. Once everyone was seated, they were surprised to see Trixie saunter into the grouping and hop up on the trunk. She took a minute for a little self-grooming, then looked up at nothing and started purring loudly.

"What's with that cat?" Matt asked.

"Is that you, Althea?" Scout said.

The ghost shimmered into view. Though the kids could all see her, it was clear her son didn't realize she was there.

"I guess you can't see her," Pekin noted.

"She's here now?" Matt asked. "Why can't I see her?"

"I think you're too, um, possibly high energy? You have to be calm inside for her to be able to get through to you."

"I'm calm," Matt said with a huff.

"We have yet to see that side of you," Amber muttered under her breath.

Tell him about me, Althea demanded.

"We will," Pekin said to the ghost. Looking at Matt, she said, "She wants us to tell you about her."

"If she's really here, ask her where I spent my eighth birthday."

It was a really fun one, Althea responded. *We took a trip to California so you could go to Disneyland.*

"Uh, Chuck E. Cheese?" Scout asked, winking at Amber.

"I knew she wasn't really there!" Matt thundered, shooting to his feet.

"I was just kidding," Scout said. "She took you to California so you could see Disneyland."

"That was mean," Pekin said.

"I couldn't help myself, Pekie," Scout said. "I'm sorry," he said to Matt.

Matt, whose eyes were wide in shock, said, "She's . . . she's really here?" He glanced around the room. "Mom?"

Tell him I'm here! the ghost said, shimmering in agitation.

"She's really here," Pekin said. "And she's frantic for you to know that."

"But . . . why is she here?"

"She's here because she loves you too much to leave," Amber blurted.

"I love her too," he responded. "But she's dead. Why is she hanging around?"

"I just *told* you," Amber said, hands on her hips, a frown of frustration on her face.

"I mean, what's her plan?" Matt asked. "Is she just visiting, or what?"

"I don't think she wants to just visit," Pekin said. "She wants to stay here until you join her in . . . in . . . wherever."

"That's a long time from now," Matt said, adding, "hopefully."

Trixie, who'd moved on to the back of the shop, was meowing. *I'll be right back.* Althea said. *She wants treats.*

In moments, the sound of kibble skittering across the floor caused Matt to glance fearfully down the aisle.

"This was her shop," he said. "Why has she been trying to destroy it?"

"I don't think she wanted to destroy it," Scout said. "That was her way of trying to get your attention. Since she couldn't announce her presence with words."

"We told her she needs to abide by your decision of whether she can stay or not," Amber said. "If you want her to move on and leave you alone, hopefully she will defer to your wishes."

Don't just tell him that! the ghost, who'd rematerialized, said. *Make him see that he needs me. Don't let him send me away.*

"We'll try," Pekin said to the air.

At least it looked like air to the flustered shop owner. "Is she here?"

"She's here," Pekin said. "And she wants us to ask you to please let her stay."

"I don't know. If she keeps breaking things I'll have to close up shop."

I won't! Althea sputtered. *I just did that so you'd notice me.*

"She only wanted you to notice her," Pekin said. "She said she won't keep breaking things."

"Maybe," Scout started, "you could set some ground rules for her to stick around."

"Like what?" the puzzled man asked.

"I don't know. Like maybe she only comes around when you don't have customers. Or she promises not to break anything else."

"Then how will I know she's there? It's not like I can speak to her."

"Maybe there can be a spot where she can let you know when she's around," Pekin said. "I mean, she'll always be around but maybe every day at, say, one o'clock you can have a cup of tea and sit with her."

"Yes!" Amber said with a grin. "Since she can break things and move things around, you can make her a cup of tea too, and she can pick up the cup and pretend like she can drink it. Then you can talk to her."

"Can you do that?" Pekin asked the ghost.

Of course, I can, the ghost replied. *That will be so much fun.*

"I'm just not sure," Matt said.

The ghost let out a wail and started to sob. And then she vanished.

"She's upset," Amber said. "Now she's crying."

"Mom?" Matt's expression was horrified. He looked at Amber. "I don't want to make her sad, but I just don't see how—"

At that moment, a cup and saucer floated toward them and settled on the steamer trunk, which was acting as a coffee table in the little seating area.

Matt's hand flew to his mouth.

"Mom? Is that you?"

As if in answer, the cup and saucer glided toward him across the steamer trunk.

"Notice that it's cold in here now?" Amber interrupted. "That's what we were talking about earlier."

Matt looked around with big eyes and buttoned the blazer he was wearing. "Now that you mention it . . ."

Amber smiled. "That's how you know."

Pekin heard a *harrumph*, and glanced at the ghost who stood smugly with her arms crossed and a satisfied grin on her face. Pekin wasn't sure she liked the glint in Althea's eyes.

"Can you ask her how it's supposed to work?" Matt said, crossing his arms and rubbing his arms up and down, apparently very aware of the temperature in the room.

"Althea, what exactly is your plan . . . your wish for how this should go?" Pekin asked.

Matt watched Pekin because he couldn't see his mother's ghost.

I just want to be near my son. If he wants to say something to me, I'd be so happy. And he'll never even know I'm here most of the time. Won't it make him happy to realize I'm close to him?

"She thinks it would make you feel content to know she's watching over you."

"I'm not sure," he said, eyebrows knitting together. "I can't have her breaking things and scaring my customers. I just don't think it's practical."

The teacup and saucer were suddenly swept off the trunk, causing everyone to jump.

That's so selfish of him. He never thought of me, only of himself.
More sobs.

"She thinks you don't care about her," Pekin said, not taking her eyes off Althea.

"Mom," he pleaded to the air. "Of course I care about you, but, if I can't even see you, then I don't see the point. Shouldn't you be going off to heaven? Or something?"

Amber shivered at the glower the ghost was exhibiting. "She's really mad."

"I don't think she's mad," Pekin said, not sure she believed it. "She just hoped her son would want her to be with him."

Tell him I won't break anything else. I only did that to get his attention. Now that he knows I'm here, I don't need to. And I promise not to make a peep while customers are around.

"She's saying she'll be on her best behavior and stop breaking things and scaring people. She said she only did that so you'd notice her."

He needs me to watch over him! I can protect him!

Pekin was tired of acting as a go-between, but didn't see any other option. "She really wants to be here with you."

Matt looked conflicted and said to Pekin, "What do *you* think I should do?"

"Gosh," Pekin said in alarm. "It's such a personal decision. I can't really make it for you. What if I make the wrong one?" She looked to her friends for help.

"How do you really feel?" Scout asked. "If you had a warm, loving relationship with your mother, you might not mind if she's still here."

"I'm not sure warm and loving——" Matt started before looking around fearfully.

"Althea," Pekin said to the ghost, who was clouding up like a thunderstorm ready to burst, "Matt has to make his own decision. You promised to abide by his decision. Not everyone would feel comfortable having a ghost in residence."

The ghost wailed loudly and disappeared.

"She left," Pekin said.

"For good?" Matt asked.

"I don't think so. It appears her feelings were hurt that you aren't jumping at the chance for her to stay by your side."

Strains of "A Dream Is a Wish Your Heart Makes" floated toward them.

"That's the player piano," Matt said. "My mother used to sing that song to me when I was a child. I haven't heard it in years."

"Um, it sounds lovely?" Amber said, unsure about the tinkly sounds, which grew louder as if someone had turned up the volume on a radio.

Pekin shivered, not sure she liked the sound.

When the song was finished, Althea shimmered back into the view of the Ghosties.

I could play the piano. Then you'd know I was here, Mattie.

"She said you'd know she was here when she played the piano. Otherwise, she'd stay out of your way."

Matt closed his eyes and shook his head. "I just don't know. What if I get married? I'm not sure my wife would be happy to have an invisible mother-in-law. There's just so much to consider."

Please, Mattie, please. I don't want to leave you. You'll hardly know I'm here. Please, Mattie.

"She's really pleading now," Amber said. "She promises to be good if you'll just let her stay."

"Why don't you think about it overnight?" Scout said. "You can meet us for lunch tomorrow and you can tell us your decision."

But I can't be there, Althea wailed.

"I think your son needs to be able to speak freely without worrying about hurting your feelings," Scout said to the ghost.

"And you should be on your best behavior the rest of the day," Amber said. "If you want him to say yes."

"That means don't be scaring him," Pekin said. "This has to be his decision." Pekin turned away from the ghost, then turned back. "And don't pout. It doesn't solve anything."

"And don't follow him home and bug him all night," Amber said.

Oh, don't worry. I'm stuck here. I can't venture outside my shop.

"Good to know," Scout said.

Humph, Althea said, and disappeared.

"How about meeting at that Mexican restaurant, Tio Taco I think it's called?" Pekin said to Matt.

"I know that one," he said. "Great salsa. And their guacamole's to die for. Noon?"

"Sure. We'll see you there at noon."

The Ghosties filed out of the shop and waited while Scout unlocked his car doors. Pekin glanced at Scout but couldn't catch his eye. On the drive home, Amber chattered away in the backseat. The only responses from her friends were their grunts or noncommittal one-syllable answers. Scout stared straight ahead while Pekin stole furtive glances his way, hoping they could talk after he dropped Amber off.

When it was obvious he intended to take Pekin home first, her stomach clenched in dread. Taking a deep breath as she stepped out of the car, she said, "Scout, I'd like to talk to you. Can you come by later? Maybe we can get a pizza or something?" She held that breath as she waited for his response.

"Actually, I'm kind of busy tonight. My mom wants me to do some stuff around the house. I'll see you tomorrow. I'll pick you guys up around eleven thirty." He flashed a smile that didn't quite reach his eyes. "Sound good?"

"Yeah, great," Pekin said through clenched teeth, having to mentally stop herself from slamming the car door. Scout had been so *normal* while they were with Matt on ghost business, but she knew he didn't intend to be his normal self when it came to her. Pekin's feelings careened between relief that Scout was friendly when they were dealing with the Althea situation and depression when he was aloof the rest of the time. Maybe he'd never forgive her for the way she acted about Vanessa Dooley.

Before she walked up the path to her front door, Pekin caught a glimpse of Amber's worried face as she climbed into the front seat of the car. Amber flashed a *call you later* sign at her as Scout pulled away from the curb.

Pekin pasted on a cheery expression when she encountered her mother in the hallway, assuring her that everything was good. She related the morning's ghostly appointment and said they were meeting their client for lunch the next day to see what he wanted to do about his mother's reluctance to leave.

Finding Griselda asleep on her bed, Pekin collapsed beside her and let silent tears fall, then turned on her side and curled around the little gray-and-white cat. Griselda's purrs made her feel a smidge better, and, after a bit, Pekin dozed off. She dreamed about Scout and Vanessa Dooley, hand in hand, walking away from her. In her dream, Vanessa Dooley looked back over her shoulder and smirked as she planted a kiss on Scout's cheek.

She awoke with a splitting headache, which she blamed for her despondent appearance at dinner and for rushing back to her room as soon as dinner was over.

Chapter Ten

PEKIN LOOKED TENTATIVELY AT Scout before greeting Amber in the backseat. Scout had smiled at her, but without that special warmth she was used to receiving from him.

"So . . . what do you guys think? Is Matt going to let Althea stay?" Amber asked. "I think he will for sure. It's all about love."

"I'm not sure about that," Scout said.

"Yeah," Pekin added. "It could go either way."

"I guess we'll find out," Scout said.

Pekin sighed and turned to look back at Amber. "I think he will. She's his mother after all. Unless he didn't like her. He didn't say that, but I get the feeling there's some undercurrent there, like maybe everything wasn't perfect all the time between them."

"Nothing's perfect all the time with anyone," Scout said, keeping his eyes straight ahead.

"No, it's not," Pekin said. "People make stupid mistakes sometimes and wish they could do it over."

He grunted. "Yeah. Sure."

Pekin and Amber exchanged a glance, and Amber mouthed *It'll be all right*, but Pekin turned around and stared out the window on the passenger side without responding.

No one spoke until Tio Taco came into view and Scout had parked the Corolla.

Pekin squared her shoulders and placed herself in Scout's path so that he had to stop and acknowledge her. "What?" he said.

"You may be mad at me. You may not want to be my boyfriend anymore, but this is business. We're going to meet our client, and I hope you can at least be civil in front of our client." She spun toward the restaurant.

"When have I ever *not* been civil in front of our client?" he responded before grabbing the restaurant door to hold open for his two buddies.

Stopping just inside, Amber put her hands on her hips and said, "Just cut it out. Whatever's going on, you guys should fix it. I feel like I have to walk on eggshells around you two."

"Oh, Amber—" Pekin started, but was cut off when Scout pointed over her shoulder. "There's Matt. He's already got a table." He brushed past Pekin, leaving Pekin and Amber looking stunned.

Amber frowned. "What a jerk. He's being—"

Her eyes widened. "Pekie, don't you dare cry. You can fix this. Come on. Matt's waving us over, and you want to look professional, don't you?"

Pekin wiped quickly at her eyes. "Do I look okay?"

Amber scrutinized her friend for a moment. "You look

fine. Now, take a deep breath, and let's go find out about Althea's future."

Matt looked defeated and uncharacteristically subdued.

"Are you okay?" Amber asked as she sat down opposite him.

"Oh yes. I just haven't been able to sleep since you brought my mother back into my life."

"We didn't bring—" Pekin started.

He waved his hand. "Oh, you know what I mean. You communicated with her. Relayed her demands."

"I think they were more like her wishes," Amber said. "I mean, she's leaving it up to you."

"You think so?" he asked. "You didn't know her. She can be overbearing and manipulative."

"So, does that mean you want her to go?" Scout asked.

"Would that be selfish of me?" Matt asked, looking sheepishly at the Ghosties.

"No," Pekin said. "It's your life now. She had hers."

"Yeah, but, if you love her and will miss her, you could still let her stay," Amber offered.

Matt shook his head. "I don't know. I really don't know. What do you think I should do?"

The three kids looked at each other. Finally, Pekin said, "We can't make that decision for you. You know what kind of relationship you and your mother had. Only you know what she meant to you." At his hangdog expression, she added, "She doesn't want to leave you. She loves you. If you decide you want her to move on, I'm pretty sure she won't be happy about it. But it's your decision."

"Did you have a good relationship with her? You know, before?" Scout asked.

Matt seemed reluctant to answer. After several moments where he chewed on his lip and scratched his chin, he said, "I guess she can stay."

"That's great!" Amber exclaimed.

Matt looked doubtful. "She could be . . . a lot . . . you know? Very strong willed."

"You sound a little afraid of her," Scout said.

Matt immediately backtracked. "Oh no. Mother was wonderful. She doted on me." But Pekin noticed something that looked like dread in his eyes.

Amber was grinning and rubbing her hands together gleefully. "Super! I can't wait to tell her. She's going to be *so* excited."

Matt scooted out of the booth and started toward the door.

"I hope Matt is," Pekin said, grabbing her bag before standing up.

"He'll be okay," Amber said. "I mean, what can happen anyway?"

"Yeah," Scout said sarcastically. "What could go wrong?"

Under her breath, Pekin muttered, "Oh, I don't know. Dishes breaking, pictures flying off the wall . . ."

Scout shot her a glance. She wasn't certain, but he might be as unsure about this as she was.

"See you there?" Pekin said to Matt at the door and watched him climb into his Suburban before following Scout and Amber to the Corolla.

CHAPTER ELEVEN

"SERIOUSLY, ALTHEA," Pekin said as all parties were gathered in the front of the shop. "There needs to be some rules. Tell her, Matt."

"Well, Mom, you won't scare off my customers, will you?"

I'll be sooo good. You'll hardly notice me.

"She says she'll be on her best behavior," Pekin translated.

"Since I can't see her, how will I know when she's around?" he asked.

"We talked about that," Amber said. "Remember? You were going to have tea at one o'clock every day?"

"Oh yeah. Tea."

"You don't like that idea?" Pekin asked.

Matt frowned. "Not really. I might get busy and forget. Can you think of anything else?"

Pekin looked at the ghost. "Well?"

"Remember, you said you wouldn't break anything, Mother," Matt said.

"Tell him, Althea," Pekin said, trying to keep the exasperation out of her voice.

I won't. I already said that.

"She won't." Pekin said and tapped a finger on her chin. "Let's see. Did your mom have a favorite perfume she wore all the time? Maybe she had a favorite flower she kept in the house? If there was a fragrance you associated with her, and if she could manifest it, maybe that could be how you knew."

"No. Mom didn't do anything like that. The only fragrances I associate with her were lemon-scented furniture polish and ammonia cleaners. Think of something else."

"Me?" Pekin squawked. "She's *your* mother."

I have an idea, Althea said. Matt couldn't hear her, so Pekin held up a finger for silence.

"She has an idea."

I can play the piano. I know he can hear that. Maybe he can sit and have a cup of tea and listen to me play.

"She says she'll play the piano, and you can have tea with her while you enjoy her playing."

"It's a player piano, so she isn't playing it," Matt groused. At Pekin's glare, he added, "But I get the idea."

Good. It's settled then. Oh, Mattie. I'm so happy!

"She's really happy you're letting her stay here," Pekin said.

"This will be weird," he said, "but we'll make it work."

"Great," Pekin said and cleared her throat. "It's been nice working with you." Spotting the ghost out of the corner of her eye, she added, "And you too, Althea."

The trio filed out of the shop and climbed into Scout's car. "I hope it all works out," Pekin said.

"You seem worried about it," Scout said. "What's going on?"

"I don't know. I just have this unsettled feeling. And, I hate to say it, but I don't like that ghost. Is that awful?"

"She is a little pushy," Amber said. "But, don't forget, the cat likes her."

"I suppose animals are good judges of character."

"Or the cat likes the treats Althea provides," Scout said.

"I could use some lunch," Pekin said. "Do you guys want to stop at Benny's on the way home?"

No one answered right away.

"It's okay if you don't want to," Pekin said, turning to look out her window.

"I'm not really feeling hungry," Scout said, right before it got awkward in the car.

Pekin smiled brightly. "No problem. I have peanut butter and jelly at home. We probably go to Benny's too often anyway."

"Maybe next time?" Amber said.

"Sure," Scout added. "We'll do it again soon."

Pekin sighed inwardly, hoping they could get past the elephant in the room. Or, in this case, the elephant in the car. Otherwise it would be a long drive home.

"CAN YOU DROP ME OFF first?" Amber asked once they were heading home. "I think you two should talk to each other."

Pekin cringed, but Scout nodded his okay, and no one spoke the rest of the trip.

She was nervous, not knowing what Scout was thinking. Or if he would forgive her. And she held her breath once Amber was out of the car.

"So, where should we go?" Scout asked.

"Can we go to the park down by Lake Brawley?" she asked, not wanting to sit in the car in front of her house. "I don't want my mom to see us and worry about me."

"Okay," Scout replied, pulling away from the curb.

When they reached the lake, Pekin followed Scout to a picnic table in the shade of a large old oak. It was a rare find, given the heat and humidity of mid-August and the number of vacationers lolling on the grass or wading at the shoreline. More than a dozen blankets were spread out across the wide expanse of lawn leading down to the lake, and music from various personal devices floated in the air.

Almost as soon as they sat down, Pekin jumped in. "I'm so sorry, Scout. I acted like a jerk. Do you hate me?"

He looked at her but didn't smile. "I don't hate you, Pekie, but I don't know if I'm ready to forgive you."

Pekin's mouth fell open, but she quickly closed it. "You don't?" she squeaked out.

"I didn't deserve the way you treated me, Pekin. And I'm not willing to take heat every time you're feeling insecure."

"Gosh, Scout. I'm not usually insecure. It's just . . . her."

"And why her? It's not like I used to date her or anything."

"You did go to the prom with her."

"I just ran into her there, and she latched on to me."

"Really?"

"Even if I did date her, I'm dating you now. What have I done to make you feel—"

"Nothing. You haven't done anything but be the best boyfriend ever." She tried a smile, but Scout just looked sad. "I promise I won't overreact again. Okay?"

Scout sighed. "Look. I suppose Vanessa does . . . flirt sometimes. She probably flirts with all the guys like that. I guess I didn't look at it from your point of view, and I can see why it would bother you."

"You didn't even—"

He held up his hand. "You're right. I should have made it clear I wasn't interested. I guess I didn't want to embarrass her. But she doesn't mean anything to me."

Scout leaned back against the picnic table and looked out over the lake. Pekin swung her legs out from under the table so that she was facing the same way, but as she reached back for her bottle of water, Scout's phone vibrated on the table, and she couldn't miss the name VANESSA that flashed on the screen. She sucked in her breath, and Scout looked around in time to see Pekin's stricken face and Vanessa's name before it vanished.

He picked up his phone and stuck it in a pocket, then looked at Pekin, waiting for her reaction.

"What? What, Pekin? Are you going to yell at me or stomp off because Vanessa happened to call?"

She sighed, her shoulders slumping. It was almost ironic that, at the very moment they were discussing her reaction to Vanessa Dooley, who should call but Vanessa Dooley. Pekin could tell that Scout would judge her on how she responded to the phone call.

"I'm not going to stomp off, and I'm not going to yell. I *do* trust you, Scout. And I'm insecure. But I promise to work on it." Pekin clasped her hands in her lap, her gaze downcast. "I hope you can forgive me."

For a moment, Scout didn't respond. Then he slid closer to her and put his arm around her shoulders. "If you can forgive me. I might have overreacted too. I don't want to be mad at you, Pekie. Vanessa was calling because—"

"You don't have to tell me. I don't want you to think you have to tell me anything you don't want to." She snuggled under his arm but didn't raise her head.

"Pekie, I want you to know. Vanessa was returning my call. I wanted to tell her that I can't help with her party decorations after all." He raised his hand before Pekin could respond. "I don't want you to feel insecure about Vanessa or anyone else. *You're* my girlfriend. My only girlfriend. And that's the way I want it to be." He tipped her chin up with his finger and kissed her as she threw her arms around his neck for a big hug.

"Oh my God, Scout! Now I can breathe again."

He laughed. "Want to reschedule last Saturday night?"

"I do. I really do." She pulled out her phone. "I have to text Amber to let her know everything's okay. You know how she worries."

"Yeah. *She* worries. Right."

She laughed and punched his arm lightly. "Well, you

know she'll be happy to know that we're all right."

"Tell her hi for me." He picked up his water bottle. "Let's go. I should probably spend a little time with my family."

"You have to hug me again first," Pekin said, looking up at him and for a moment considering batting her eyelashes like Vanessa Dooley would. Thankfully, common sense prevailed, and she giggled at the thought.

"Why are you laughing?" Scout asked as he pulled her into a bear hug.

"I'm just happy, that's all," she said, burying her face in his chest. She then pushed away and looked up at him with a grin. "Race you to the car."

CHAPTER TWELVE

~~~~~~

IT WAS ONLY A WEEK LATER that Matt Cooley called Pekin. The hair on the back of her neck stood up. It couldn't be good that he was calling so soon.

"How are things going with your mom?" she asked.

"Um," he paused. "Um," he said again. She could hear stress in his voice, and she was worried the Ghosties were about to get their first customer service complaint. Maybe he wasn't calling just to give a status update.

Pekin's concern mounted. "Why did you call? Did something happen? It hasn't been that long. Is she—"

"Would it be possible for you to come by the shop when you have a moment?" Matt's voice was uncharacteristically shaky.

"Sure. I'll check with Scout and Amber. If they're available, we can probably stop by this afternoon. How about two o'clock? If they don't have other plans, we'll be there."

"Thank you."

Texting Scout and Amber, she relayed Matt's request to see them, and Scout said he'd pick them up around one-thirty.

Pekin's nerves caused her to babble all the way to the shop. About never trusting that ghost, about hoping Althea hadn't hurt Matt, about how unexpected the whole situation was.

Scout tried to convince her that everything was fine but finally gave up and let her vent until they pulled up in front of the shop.

Matt opened the front door before they were even out of the car.

Pekin let out a gasp. Matt looked . . . different. His eyes were sunken and rimmed with dark circles. His hair was in disarray, and he looked exhausted.

She could tell by glancing at Scout that he'd noticed the same thing. Once they were inside, she said, "Matt, have you been sick? You don't look well."

"I don't feel so well. I don't know what's wrong with me."

"Have you seen a doctor?" Scout asked.

"Um, no. I think it's her." He indicated the air, meaning his mother.

"Why would you—"

Hellooo, a ghostly voice said, and Althea materialized in front of them. She was looking . . . vibrant . . . if you could say that about a shimmering entity. There was almost color in her face, and even her pink tracksuit seemed brighter. She appeared to be more solid.

Pekin's stomach dropped, concerned at the thought that there was a connection between the two changes in appearance.

"You look . . . well." Pekin said to the ghost.

I feel great! she gushed. *Life . . . pardon me, I mean death . . . has been wonderful. Mattie and I are having just the best time.*

Matt's eyes were focused on a shimmer in the air, his eyes wide. "Is that her?" He was pointing at Althea.

"You can see her?" Pekin said.

"Not really. There's just *something* there. It's vague, though. What did she say?"

"She said everything is wonderful here. Is that true, Matt?" Scout asked.

Matt looked like he was afraid to answer, and Pekin wondered where his blustery Type A personality had disappeared to. "Well, I, um, I guess so."

Oh, tell them, Mattie. We've been having fun. Althea seemed to darken, and Amber backed up.

"Are you haunting your son?" Amber asked. "He doesn't look so good."

He just worries too much. Everything is peachy keen with us. She glared at her son, whose shoulders were hunched, his eyes scanning the room, not sure where the ghost was. He started to shiver as the temperature dropped sharply.

"Why are you making it so cold in here?" Pekin asked.

Because I can, she cackled, and vanished. Within moments, the strains of "A Dream Is a Wish Your Heart Makes" floated in the air.

"She plays that over and over. All day long. It's driving me out of my mind."

"Have you asked her to stop or to play something else?" Pekin asked.

"I've talked to the piano. I can't see her, you know. But, yes. I asked her nicely. Then I asked nicely again, and then I sort of yelled at her. Mother has a strong will. She never listened to me when she was alive."

"I'm so sorry to hear that," Pekin said, looking helplessly at her friends.

"Well, can you do something about it?"

"We can talk to her, see if she'll be reasonable about it." Rolling her shoulders back, she turned to Scout and Amber. "Let's go." She marched back toward the player piano, followed by her friends.

Finding Althea pretending to play along to the music, Pekin said, "Althea, you can't play that all the time. It's driving your son crazy."

The ghost cackled again, and the volume grew louder.

Pekin put her hands on her hips and scowled at Althea. "I mean it. You have to be considerate of your son's wishes. You agreed to play by the rules."

The volume went up again, and the kids and Matt put their hands over their ears and rushed away from the piano.

"See what I mean?" Matt said. "You have to do something. I can't stand this."

Pekin spun around and stomped back to the piano. "Althea, I think Matt wants to change his mind. You're not being very nice. This isn't working out. You have to go."

Make me.

Pekin was shocked at Althea's almost-threatening response.

Without looking up from the piano, the ghost added, *I don't think you can. Now run along.*

Pekin's mouth hung open, but nothing came out of it. She shut it, turned on her heels, and went back to join her friends at the front of the shop.

"What did she say?" Matt asked.

"I think we're going to have a problem. She thinks she's the boss. She told me to run along."

Matt looked stricken. "But if you can't do anything . . . ."

"We need to talk to our friend Mildew. She'll know what to do," Pekin said.

"Mildew?"

"Mildew Willingham. She's our mentor."

"Yeah," Amber added. "She'll know what to do."

"We'll meet with her right away and get back to you."

"What do I do until then?" Matt said, wringing his hands. "I can't stand this."

"Maybe," Scout said, "if you play nice with her, she'll at least turn down the volume. Go take a cup of tea . . . take two of them . . . offer one to her and sit down by the piano. Apologize and say how much you love having her around. We'll try to be fast and get back to you as soon as we can."

Matt's downcast expression was his only response.

"Okay, then. Maybe you should close up shop for the day and go home," Scout said. "Give her a chance to cool off."

"Yeah, that might be a good idea. We'll see you as soon as we know something," Pekin said, waving goodbye. She was already texting Mildew as they got in the car.

When her phone dinged, Pekin glanced at it and then

up at her friends. "She said we can come over now."

"I hope Mildew knows what to do," Amber said. "If she doesn't, well, then we're kind of in a pickle."

"In a pickle?" Pekin laughed. "Do people even say that anymore?"

"I couldn't think of a better word," Amber said.

Chapter Thirteen

~~~~~~

MILDEW WILLINGHAM WAS A small, round woman, who sometimes brought to mind Tangina Barrons, the odd little medium in the original *Poltergeist* movie. Without the squeaky voice. Mildew had been drawn by her spirit guides to the house at 12 Elmwood that had been the Ghosties' first case. It was a good thing, too, as the trio had been in way over their heads. Pekin was snatched away by the evil ghost who tormented the spirit of Miranda, the teenage girl he'd murdered a century before. Without Mildew's help, and the knowledge she brought with her, the outcome might have been tragic. Instead, Pekin was rescued, Miranda was set free, and George Trent was sent on his way to whatever awaited him in the great beyond.

The kids remained friends with Mildew, and she was happy to help them develop their abilities for dealing with the spirit world. It was Mildew who pointed out how important it was to meditate—to clear and calm their minds—so that spirits would have an easier time connecting with them.

She was waiting at her front door when they arrived and gave hugs all around.

"What can I help you with?" she asked.

"Remember I told you about our latest client?" Pekin began. "The ghost haunting his store turned out to be his mother. And she doesn't want to leave."

"Have you—"

Pekin held up her hand and was immediately embarrassed at cutting the medium off in the middle of a sentence. "Sorry. I didn't mean to interrupt."

"It's okay, dear. You can tell it in your own way."

"It's just that we're really worried. The ghost said she wanted to stick around because she couldn't bear to be separated from her son. After some negotiations, Matt decided it was okay for her to stay."

"But he looks really different now," Amber interjected. "He looks . . . haunted."

"Yes. Haunted is a good word," Pekin said. "And I don't think he's happy with the bargain. She's being obnoxious. Today, she got mad at us when we said she needed to leave, and she started playing the player piano so loud that the walls shook. Can we get her to cross over if she doesn't want to?"

"Hmm." Mildew tilted her head as she pondered the question. "There are things we can try. One thing that is often effective is to demand the spirit leave and then ignore it if it doesn't, since ignoring it deprives it of energy."

"You mean like starving it?"

"Exactly. A spirit entity can't feed off itself. It can just exist. But when an energy source is present, a motivated spirit can absorb some of that energy to make itself stronger. More there."

"I don't think Matt's the kind of guy who could do that effectively," Pekin said. "He's too antsy and nervous."

"That wouldn't be helpful," Mildew agreed. "All that nervous energy would probably feed the spirit."

"I just don't understand why she would do this. She told us she loved her son," Amber said.

"I think Althea . . . that's the ghost . . . has a diabolical plan," Scout said. "I think she wants to make herself solid enough to come back, no matter what it does to her son."

"Weird, since she can't leave the antique shop," Pekin said.

"It's actually helpful that she can't leave, since your client isn't being chased from his home."

"Have you heard of a ghost doing that? Getting stronger by making the person it's haunting weaker?" Scout asked.

"I've heard of it," Mildew said, "but I haven't run across that scenario myself."

"What if we can't make her leave?" Amber asked. "Maybe we should get Miranda's input on this." She looked at Pekin. "Can you call her?"

Pekin closed her eyes and made a silent request for their ghost friend to appear. Within moments, the air shimmered, and a fairly solid-looking Miranda joined them, wearing a mirror image of Pekin's outfit—white shorts and a light blue T-shirt with white stars.

"She's dressed like you today," Amber noted. "I guess you look better than I do."

You look nice, too, Amber. I just like stars.

"I was kidding, Miranda. You can wear whatever you like."

I've been having so much fun. I've been to Paris! When I was alive, I never traveled from my hometown. But Paris! The museums——

"Miranda, we'd love to catch up with you, but we need your help," Scout said.

"We have this weird thing going on with our new client. His mother is the ghost," Pekin said. "She says she wants to stay because she loves her son so much, but I don't think it's good for him. He's starting to look sick. Circles around his eyes, losing weight, paler."

"She's a domineering presence," Scout added. "Very strong willed."

"And I think he's afraid of her," Amber said. "We came to see if Mildew would know how to make her leave."

"It's only been a week," Pekin said. "If he looks that bad in a week, I'm afraid to see what will happen to him in a month."

Miranda shimmered, becoming vaguer and then more solid, clearly agitated. *She's draining him.*

"That's what I thought, too," Mildew said.

"What does that mean?" Amber asked.

She's like a vampire, but, instead of blood, she's drinking all his energy. His essence.

"I suppose the ghost is looking . . . better?" Mildew asked.

"Now that you mention it, she's practically glowing," Pekin said.

If you don't stop her, he'll just become weaker and weaker, until he almost fades away. This is troubling.

"What can we do?" Pekin asked.

"Do you know why she haunts that place?" Mildew asked.

"Well, it was her store. Her son inherited it after she died."

"Still—"

"We don't know what happened to her," Scout said. "Maybe she died there?"

"I'll text Matt and ask him," Pekin said, pulling out her phone.

"That's a good idea," Mildew said. "If we can pin down all the circumstances, it might help us decide on a plan of action."

Pekin's phone dinged, and she read through the message. "He said she had a heart attack. In the shop."

"But you're sure she's confined there?" Mildew asked.

"When we were negotiating her terms, I mentioned something about his house, and she said she couldn't leave the shop."

"We can try to sage the shop," Mildew said. "That might make her uncomfortable enough that she will decide to leave on her own. Is there somewhere in the shop she goes most often?"

"I'm not sure, but the arrangement we made for her to let her son know she was near was that she would play the piano, and, when he heard the music, he could go have a cup of tea with her. He can't really see her or hear her. I think because he's too Type A."

"That means he's always rushing around, and his brain is busy, Miranda," Amber said.

"If the sage isn't effective, we can put a circle of salt around the piano when she's playing it. She'll be trapped in that small area," Mildew said.

"Won't she see us spreading the salt and go somewhere else?"

"That is a concern. I would suggest preparing enough of the circle, starting at the back and leaving just the front open, so that if the three of you work together you can close the circle before she can escape."

Pekin was skeptical, her eyebrows drawing together in a slight frown. "Sounds kind of iffy."

"Nothing is certain in this business," Mildew said. "We can only do our best."

"I don't think our best will be satisfactory to Matt if we can't get the ghost out," Pekin said.

"I think you should start by talking to the ghost and explaining the situation isn't working out and that she needs to go. If she refuses, you can threaten to use the sage. See how she reacts, and be ready to smudge the store. You remember how to do it?"

"I do," Amber said. "It was kind of fun."

"If you hold your breath," Scout noted, comically pinching his nose.

CHAPTER FOURTEEN

"WHY DID YOU LEAVE Trixie at home?" Pekin asked when they met Matt the next morning. "We have an idea of how to deal with the ghost, and the cat might have helped since Althea likes her."

"Not anymore, she doesn't," he responded. "At least, Trixie doesn't like my mom. Trixie finds a hiding spot as soon as I bring her in, so I've been leaving her home."

"Althea's quiet so far this morning," Scout noted. "Maybe we should talk outside in case she's eavesdropping."

Matt frowned but led them back out the front door. "What's your idea?"

"A couple of things. First, we brought sage with us and we're going to sage the whole shop. That seems to make ghosts uncomfortable."

"And if that doesn't work," Amber said, "we're going to try to trap her at the piano with salt."

"Great," Matt said with a grimace. "She'll be stuck in the place where she can drive me nuts with the piano playing."

"Maybe we can take the rolls out? Does it plug in?"

"It does plug in, but it can also be played using the pedals. It's complicated. But we *can* take out the rolls," Matt said.

"The thing is," Pekin said, "we need some kind of distraction so she doesn't notice us as we spread the salt around. But, for now, let's see how far we get with saging."

Scout got the sack with the smudge sticks, bundles of dried sage stems bound together with cotton thread, and abalone shells out of his car trunk. He handed one shell and one bundle of sage to Pekin and one of each to Amber. "Do you want to wait out here for us to do this?" he asked Matt. "It might make her mad."

Matt shivered. "I think I will. Thanks."

When the Ghosties started wandering around the shop with the lighted smudge sticks, at first there was no sign of Althea, but as the aroma of the sage started to permeate the interior, an angry ghost appeared in an aisle in front of Pekin.

What are you doing? Althea waved her arms wildly. *Stop it immediately.*

"I don't think so, Althea," Pekin said. "You can't stay here anymore. You're draining your son, and that wasn't part of the bargain. He only let you stay here because you said you loved him too much to leave him. Obviously, that was a lie. If you loved your son, you wouldn't be endangering him."

Well, I don't intend to leave. Sprinkle your smelly fragrance all over the shop. See if I care.

The Ghosties continued with the smudging. They spread out to the corners of the store, each carrying a smudge stick and an abalone shell to contain the ashes and sparks from the burning sage. Each used a feather to waft the smoke into corners and toward the ceiling so that the entire store was soon blanketed in the smell of the smoke.

Stop it! Stop it right now! the spirit growled. *It's nasty, and I don't like it.*

"This is only the beginning if you don't leave, Althea," Pekin said.

A sudden burst of ghostly laughter filled the air, and the walls almost shook when she yelled, *DO YOUR WORST!*

Everyone shivered. "Let's get out of here," Scout said.

Once they'd joined Matt in front of the antique shop, he bombarded them with questions.

"Your mother wasn't happy," Pekin said. "She laughed at us and dared us to get rid of her."

"Well, can you?" Matt asked.

"We hope so. The smell of the sage was strong, and we want to give it a chance to dissipate. Then we'll go back in there."

"What's the next step?" Matt asked.

"We want to try to trap her in a small area with salt. Since the space around the piano is where she hangs out, and we don't want her to be able to play the piano for eternity, we hope she won't be there when we go back in. What we want is for you to gather up all the piano rolls, including the one in the piano, and take them outside. While you're doing that, we're going to make a line of salt around the piano, leaving about a quarter of it open so she can get in. Once she's at the piano, we'll quickly spread salt in the remaining open space. She'll be trapped."

"Hmm," Matt said, frowning. "So many things could go wrong."

"Well, of course they could," Amber said, hands on hips. "This isn't going to be a walk in the park. We're dealing with a *dead* person. We don't know all the rules for dealing with a dead person. We're making this up as we go."

"*That* gives me a lot of comfort," Matt muttered. "I don't have to pay you the rest of your fee if you don't get rid of her, do I?"

"*Really?*" Amber huffed. "You're worried about having to pay us?" She turned toward the street. "I'm going for a walk."

"I'll go with you," Pekin said.

"Me too," Scout added. "We'll be back in half an hour. And if we can't get rid of your mother, we don't *want* your money."

Matt stood with his mouth open as he watched them walk away, but none of the Ghosties looked back.

"I don't like that man," Amber grumbled when they were out of his earshot. "He's just obnoxious."

"I can't wait until this job is over," Pekin agreed. "Our other clients have been so nice."

"That's just how business is," Scout, always the practical one, said. "There are nice clients and not-so-nice clients. Sometimes, we'll just have to gulp and do our jobs. It appears that Matt is in the second group."

"I don't even want to help him," Amber said, her eyebrows drawn together in a tight scowl.

Pekin looped her arm through Amber's. "I kinda feel the same way, but we're committed now. Let's try to wrap it up as quickly as we can."

"We might need Mildew if we can't get Althea to leave."

"Maybe," Pekin said. "But I hope not. We need to rely on ourselves."

Scout looked at his phone. "Let's head back. The smoke should be gone by now."

Matt was still grumbling when they got back to the shop, and the frown on his face deepened as they approached.

Amber's death-ray eyes were lasered in on him, and Pekin tried to stand in front of her so he wouldn't notice.

"Are you ready to grab all those piano rolls if there's no sign of your mom?" Scout asked Matt.

"Yes. Let's get this over with."

They tiptoed into the shop, hoping not to alert Althea to their presence. The shop was normal room temperature, and all four breathed sighs of relief.

Matt's hands shook as he fumbled the roll out of the player piano, pointing to the other rolls for Scout to gather. They then carried them outside and stashed them in Matt's SUV.

Pekin and Amber, each armed with a box of salt, shook a thick line around the piano, close to the base so it wouldn't be very noticeable, leaving the space in front of the instrument clear.

Once finished, they gathered outside the shop and congratulated themselves on their success.

"Should we go back inside and wait for Althea to show up?" Pekin asked.

"She's going to freak out when she tries to play the piano," Amber said. "What if she won't go into the salt circle when she finds out?"

"That could be a problem," Pekin said. "We need something to distract her so she doesn't leave before we can close the circle. Any ideas?"

"Maybe Miranda can help," Scout said. "I can't imagine Althea would be super thrilled about another ghost in her space."

"Miranda?" Matt asked. "Who's that?"

"Our ghost friend," Pekin said.

"You have a ghost friend?"

"Yes. She was our first ghost. We rescued her from the house she'd been trapped in for a hundred years."

"But she's still here? So you failed?"

"No," Scout said. "We didn't fail. She had missed out on so much that she wanted to see what the world was like now. She's only fourteen."

"But she's still here."

"We *know* she's still here, and we're fine with that. She's a sweet, fun ghost, and she can stick around as long as she wants to," Amber said. "She's not bothering anyone."

"Let's call her," Pekin said, clutching her box of salt. "Can you fix two cups of tea so you can coax your mother to come out?"

Everyone tiptoed back inside, and, while Matt busied himself in the small kitchenette putting tea bags in cups and adding hot water from the water cooler, Pekin stepped outside to beckon Miranda.

When the spirit appeared, Pekin said, "Are you worried about confronting Althea?"

I'm not sure.

"You know you can leave and she can't, right?"

That does make it better. The ghost straightened her shoulders. *I think I'm ready now.*

Amber poked her head out the door to say Matt had brought the tea out.

"Got your salt, Amber?" Pekin asked.

"Sure do," she replied, holding up her box of salt and shaking it.

Miranda ducked out of sight behind an armoire, far enough away that the spot of cold that always surrounded her wouldn't be immediately noticeable to the ghost of Matt's mother. Pekin had suggested a code word to let Miranda know it was time for her to do her part.

Once they'd taken their places on each side of the piano, trying to make the line of salt hard to spot, Matt called out to the ghost.

"Mother, I've brought us tea. Could we visit a minute?"

Althea didn't appear for several moments, so Matt tried again. "Mother, the tea is getting cold. Should I start without you?"

The chill in the room preceded her arrival. She floated over to the piano stool and glared at her son. *What are you trying to pull, Mattie? I know you don't want me around.*

"She's here," Pekin said. "She thinks you're trying to put one over on her."

"That's not true, Mother," he said, lifting his teacup in

the direction of the piano. "Perhaps we can work this all out. I thought you'd enjoy having tea with me."

Althea looked skeptically at the cup of tea sitting on the covered keyboard. *How do I know you're not trying to poison me?*

"Oh my God, Althea," Amber said with an eye roll. "You're already dead. He can't poison you."

"She thinks I'm trying to poison her?" Matt asked in surprise. "Mother, please, just have some tea and sit with me awhile."

Althea glared, although Matt was oblivious to her agitation until she swept the teacup and saucer off the piano and flipped up the cover. He cringed as the cup and saucer smashed into the corner of a dresser and shattered into a million pieces.

At the same moment Althea noticed that no sound was coming out of the piano, Pekin said, "I could use a *peanut butter* sandwich about now," the code to summon Miranda.

Miranda shimmered into view standing at the back of the piano, outside of the salt line, and Althea slammed her hands down on the keys and leaned forward toward the unwelcome ghost.

You can't be here, Althea screeched. *This is my shop. Get out! Get out NOW!*

Althea was so focused on Miranda that she wasn't aware of Pekin and Amber completing the salt circle.

You don't belong here, either, Miranda said. *It's time for you to move on. You're not wanted here.*

How dare you? Althea seethed. *I'll—*

You'll what? Miranda swept her arm out. *Look around you,*

Althea. You're trapped. Leaving is your only option now.

"Miranda's so *brave*," Amber whispered to Pekin.

"I know," Pekin whispered back.

Althea whirled around, and her gaze fell on the salt line circling the piano. *You can't do this to me! Let me out. Let me out. Let me out!* She stamped her foot and shook her fists, but she couldn't cross the salt line. *Mattie, don't let them do this to me. I'm your mother!*

"She's upset about being trapped," Pekin said. "She's begging you to let her out."

Matt stared at the piano bench, straining to see any indication of his mother. He cleared his throat. "You were being unreasonable, Mother," he said timidly. "You weren't following the rules like you promised."

Pekin watched him, concerned about the way he was rattled by his mother's spirit.

I don't have to follow your stupid rules. I'll get you for this. She shook her fist at her son and then flung her arms, attempting to sow destruction through the shop.

Nothing happened. Althea scrunched up as if marshalling all her energy, and her arms flew out again. Again, nothing happened except that the pages of the sheet music open on the piano ruffled in the wind she created.

The screech of frustration that came from her caused the kids to cover their ears.

Matt couldn't tell what was happening, but his eyes grew big seeing the way his ghost hunters cringed, ears covered. "What's going on? What happened?"

Pekin straightened up to address him. "Your mother is

trying to break things, but her energy can't get out of the salt line. I think you should be safe from her now, as long as you don't break the line."

"You mean forever?" he asked, frowning. "Customers will be shopping here. What if one of them scuffs up the salt?"

"We hope not forever," she responded. "What we want to happen is for your mother to get tired of being trapped with nowhere to go and decide to give up and cross over."

Not likely, the ghost responded.

Pekin glared at her. "Meanwhile, you should find some of those poles with velvet ropes used to keep people in line and arrange them around the piano area. Maybe put up a sign that says 'No Touching.'"

"She may not be gone yet," Scout said, "but she can't break things in the store, and you can't see her or hear her, so maybe you can go about your business and let things get back to normal."

"I'm not comfortable with this," Matt grumbled.

"Good grief, Matt," Amber said, shaking her head in exasperation. "We're doing our best. Your mother is a pain in the . . . the . . . *bottom*."

Pekin had held her breath over how Amber would finish the sentence, then sighed in relief. "She's right," Pekin said. "We're not magicians. Your mother is being difficult and we're trying to come up with the best solution possible. Can't you just see how this goes for a few days? Then, if it feels like you can't deal, we'll dig deep and try something else."

"Okay. Fine."

"Thank you. Keep us posted, and we'll call you in a couple of days to check in."

You can't leave me here like this! Althea shrieked. *Don't you dare! You'll be sorry!*

"Ta-ta, Althea," Amber said with a little wave. "Behave yourself."

"Let's go," Scout said, herding his friends out the front door. "I could use some tacos."

The three were somber on the ride to Tio Taco. Despite what they'd told Matt, it felt like they'd failed.

CHAPTER FIFTEEN

~~~~~~

"**I**'M NERVOUS LEAVING MATT there with Althea," Pekin said, dipping a chip into the chunky red salsa.

"I'm a little worried too," Scout said. "She's devious. I don't trust her."

"But what can we do?" Amber asked, breaking a big chip in half before dipping it.

Pekin rested her head in her hands for a moment, then sat up and smiled. "I have an idea. Let's see if Miranda will hang out there and keep an eye on Althea. She can let us know if anything goes wrong."

"Do you think she'll do it?" Amber asked.

"I think so. She wanted to be a Ghostie, after all. This is a chance for her to really be part of the team."

"See if you can get her," Scout said.

The kids had purposely asked for a booth in the back of the restaurant and picked a U-shaped one that seemed the most private. Pekin glanced around to make sure they were alone, and said, "Miranda, can you come talk to us?"

A shimmer appeared in an empty space on the booth

bench between Amber and Scout, and Miranda was suddenly among them.

I'm here.

"What did you think of Althea?" Pekin asked. "She's pretty obnoxious, don't you think?"

I think she's a problem. The way she's developed her ability to pull in energy is not good.

"That's what we're worried about," Amber said. "We don't think Matt is safe around her, even with her trapped at the piano."

"Which is why we called you," Pekin said. "We wondered . . . would you consider hanging out at the shop and keeping an eye on Matt to make sure he's okay?"

"You could let us know if he's in trouble," Amber said.

"It's a real Ghostie job," Pekin added. "Do you think you'd want to do that?"

"We told Matt we'd check back in with him in a few days, but he's nervous, and we're nervous for him," Scout said.

Miranda grinned happily. *I can do that. I'm so excited to be a real Ghostie!*

"Miranda, we've always considered you a Ghostie! We just didn't need your help before now." Pekin visibly relaxed her tense shoulders. "We'll feel better knowing you're watching out for Matt."

I'm on it, Miranda said before vanishing.

The mood at the table lightened considerably, and the kids finished their lunches and headed for home.

Now, they would just have to wait.

CHAPTER SIXTEEN

WRITING IN HER JOURNAL, Pekin had included her budding feelings for Scout, and many of her entries explored those feelings. They'd begun slowly at first, and she'd been a bundle of embarrassment on their first date. Where she and Scout had been inseparable friends since second grade, suddenly their conversations were stilted and nervous. Pekin had to make a special effort to overcome her nerves and allow that friendship to morph into a boyfriend-girlfriend thing. Partly . . . mostly . . . because of Scout, she'd been able to move forward after that traumatic Elmwood Manor experience, and she'd slowly grown comfortable with him.

The only hiccup in their relationship was that unfortunate incident with Vanessa Dooley. Pekin had written pages and pages to get out the upsetting feelings she'd experienced after finding her nemesis flirting with Scout right in front of her own home. It was through the process of keeping a journal that she was able to let go of her anger and realize how unfair she'd been to Scout. Thankfully, everything was good between them again.

And now here was the ghost of Althea, and once again Pekin was feeling off-kilter, unsure of herself. What if they couldn't get rid of her? Pekin felt at a loss for what to do if Althea called their bluff and decided not to budge from the shop.

Pekin's natural optimism refused to let her believe they would fail, and her journal entry ended with her assuring herself that soon, Althea would be a thing of the past.

CHAPTER SEVENTEEN

T HE TEENS HAD NO PLANS for going back to the antique shop that day. It wasn't especially pleasant listening to Matt complain about their lack of success in getting his mother to cross over. They'd see him soon enough in another day or two when they checked in to see if Althea had caved.

Pekin wanted to clean out her closet in preparation for clothes shopping for the new school year, which would start in a few weeks. She and Amber texted back and forth as Amber prepared to tackle her own closet, and they made plans to hit the mall on the weekend.

Scout, who was on the high school football team . . . *Go Tigers! . . .* was spending the morning at the gym, lifting weights and running on the track, to get himself into playing shape. He'd been on the JV team his sophomore year and had moved up to the varsity team last year. Amber's boyfriend, Josh Parker, was also on the team. Practices would be starting soon, and the Ghosties planned that their current ghost, Althea, would be their last for the year.

Pekin was still at it, surrounded by piles of shorts and

T-shirts and shoes, when the room became cool and Miranda appeared. The ghost's face was pale . . . er. Paler than usual. Pekin immediately knew there was a problem.

"What's wrong, Miranda?" she asked.

You must hurry. Althea is sucking up all of Mr. Cooley's life force.

"What do you mean? Did she get loose from the salt?"

No. But she's going to make him disappear.

"How can she make him disappear?"

She wants to be real again. She's using his energy to grow stronger. When she has as much strength as she needs, she will convince him to invite her in, and she'll live in his body.

"Oh no! That can happen? What do we do?"

You must convince Mr. Cooley to stop going near her.

"You mean he's spending a lot of time near the piano?"

No. He stays away from her, but her will is becoming over-powering for him, and soon she'll begin to worm her way into his mind and . . . You understand what I'm saying?

Pekin shuddered. She understood. George Trent had inhabited her mind, not by slowly wheedling his way into her thoughts but by taking over. The experience had filled her nights with horrible dreams for weeks following her rescue, so she was alarmed by Miranda's report.

"I'll text Scout and Amber to come over and we'll try to come up with a plan. Mildew should be here too. Maybe she'll have some ideas."

Pekin waited for her friends in the family room, alternately pacing and rushing to the window to see if they'd arrived yet, and did her best not to let her anxiety take over. What if they were already too late to save Matt?

This ghostbusting stuff was so much more complex than she'd ever imagined. She'd expected it to be maybe not exactly easy but at least understandable. After all, ghosts should *want* to go into the light. Why were so many of them dragging their feet?

Mildew brought her go-to supplies and arranged them on the large leather ottoman in Pekin's family room.

"Can you help us?" Pekin asked the petite medium after filling Mildew in on the latest events.

"Unfortunately for Matt," Mildew said, "from what you've told me, he needs to stay completely away from the store. I know he's not going to be happy to hear that, but he's providing the ghost with an ongoing supply of energy. If he's not there, it's possible she'll eventually give up."

"But it's his business," Amber said.

"I understand that," Mildew said, "but he has to balance that against his *life*."

She held up a short, stout white candle. "This is to repel the spirit. White candles provide positive energy to counter-act the negative energy your ghost is putting out. I've also brought cedar incense. It's a powerful scent that is unwelcoming to spirits. More powerful than sage."

"Do you think they'll work?" Amber asked. "She's really strong."

"That's my hope. Your client needs to speak firmly to her and tell her she's not welcome, that she needs to leave. If he projects strength and fearlessness, she may accept that she has no place on this plane of existence."

"But Matt isn't strong *or* fearless," Pekin said. "Even if he tries to put on an act of being brave, as soon as he's alone with her again, he'll cave."

"Hmm," Mildew said, resting her chin in her hand. "The three of you will need to stand with him when he confronts her then. And, I repeat, your client must immediately leave the shop and stay away from it."

"I guess we should go check it out," Scout said. "Can we borrow your candle, Mildew?"

"Of course." She offered the candle, then paused and shook several black crystals out of her bag. "These are onyx and obsidian. Both minerals are powerful in absorbing negative energy and dissipating it into the earth. Even better, they help prevent the drain of energy if a person is the focus of a malevolent spirit. Scatter these crystals near the cedar incense to interrupt the energy vibrations your ghost is sending out to entrap your client. And, remember, I'm only a phone call away if you should need me."

"Thanks, Mildew," Pekin said. "Here goes nothing."

"Now, Pekin dear, you must believe in yourself. The three of you have grown so much in your abilities and understanding of this shadowy world. Chin up. All will be okay."

CHAPTER EIGHTEEN

THE TEENS WERE IMMEDIATELY taken aback by their client's . . . deterioration. What else could they call it? Matt's eyes were sunken, and there were dark circles surrounding them. His clothes seemed to hang off his increasingly thin frame. And maybe most disturbing was the haunted look on his face. His eyes were almost empty, and the skin on his face sagged. It was like he'd given up fighting against the ghostly toll his mother was taking on him.

"Matt, what happened to you?" Pekin asked in alarm. "You look like you haven't slept in days. How late did you stay here yesterday?"

"I didn't go home. I had to stay here with Mother."

"What? You can't *do* that!"

"She needs me. I know that now."

Scout pulled Pekin aside and motioned for Amber. "Let's talk outside."

Amber was wringing her hands, worry causing her eyes to grow large. "Oh my God,." she whispered. "She's won."

Pekin shook her head. "No, she hasn't. We won't let her.

Matt's not in his right mind, and we have to rescue him."

"I agree with Pekin," Scout said. "I don't think he's going to be able to confront his mother. He's too far gone. It's up to us."

Pekin jiggled the bag of Mildew's tools and reached inside. When she withdrew her hand, she held the small black crystals meant to absorb and dispel negative energy. "I'm going to make Matt carry these around in his pocket. Mildew thinks they'll help, and we need any advantage we can get."

"Let's go talk to him again," Scout said, holding open the front door of the shop.

They didn't see him immediately when they entered but heard his voice and headed down the aisle leading to the piano. He held a cup of tea and balanced on the edge of a chair just outside the line of salt.

"I'm just thankful she hasn't yet convinced him to break the salt line," Pekin whispered behind her hand.

"Yeah," Scout whispered back.

Althea chortled in ghostly laughter at their concerned faces. *I don't think you're needed here any longer*, she said. *Mattie and I are getting along just fine. Why don't you all run along.*

"I don't think so, Althea," Pekin said. "We're just getting started."

"Matt, can we talk to you a minute?" Scout asked, taking Matt's arm.

"But, Mother—"

"Your mother is just fine. This will only take a minute."

Matt looked back and forth between the piano bench

and Scout. "I can hear her now, you know," he said. "She talks to me."

"Really," Scout said. "This will just take a minute, but it's important."

Reluctantly, Matt allowed Scout to lead him to the front of the store and then out the door.

"What—" Matt started, his head turning as Pekin and Amber joined them outside.

"You don't look well," Pekin said, putting a hand on his arm. "Please. You need to go home and get some rest."

"I can't leave Mother," he said, his eyes hardening stubbornly.

"Your mother would want you to take care of yourself," Amber said. "Wouldn't she? I mean, she loves you and wouldn't want you to get sick or anything."

Matt's eyebrow quirked up as he considered her words. "But—"

"We'll keep your mother company until you feel better," Scout said. "But you look like warmed-over pizza—"

"That's not a good example," Amber said. "Warmed-over pizza is great."

"Amber, you're missing the point," Pekin said.

"Okay, warmed-over, um . . . dang it, Amber," Scout said. "You threw me off."

Amber pulled her head down into her shoulders. "Sorreee."

"Anyway, Matt, you're not looking good."

Matt looked doubtful but said, "Let me go get my keys."

"I'll get them for you," Pekin said. "They're by your front counter, right?"

"Yes, in the slide-open compartment."

"You'll feel much better after you've gotten some rest," Scout said.

Before Matt got into his car, Pekin handed him several of the black crystals. He looked at them with a confused look on his face.

"These are good for getting rid of bad energy. Clearing the air, sort of," Pekin said. "Anyway, we think you should keep these on you all the time. Just for a while. In a pocket or something. We really believe you'll start to feel better if you do."

Matt watched as she dropped the stones into his hand. He slipped them into his pocket with a nod, and, within moments, he was in his car driving away.

"Oh God," Pekin said. "This is worse than we thought. It's like she's eating him alive."

"Well, let's go deal with the evil Althea Cooley," Scout said.

"Can we say a prayer first?" Amber asked. "Mildew said to always protect ourselves."

"Sounds good to me," Pekin said. "We could use some divine help." She grabbed her friends' hands, and Pekin spoke softly in a prayer for protection. Then the kids squared their shoulders and followed Scout into the shop.

WHERE'S MY SON? loudly greeted them when they were inside again. The spirit's shrieking led them to the piano where they carefully stayed on the outside of the salt line.

"You're destroying your son," Pekin said. "How could you?"

Oh, go blow, the ghost responded.

"I don't think we will," Pekin said. "You'll be the one who blows. Away. Blow away."

Althea laughed, but there was a hesitation to her ghostly voice, as if she wasn't totally sure she had the upper hand.

Mattie? she called loudly.

"We sent him home," Scout said. "He's not looking well."

"Yeah," Pekin said. "You wouldn't know anything about that now, would you?"

You can't beat me, you know. Althea puffed out her chest and crossed her arms. *I can outwait you.*

"Think so?" Amber challenged, her hands in fists at her sides.

Pekin held up a hand. "Let's get started."

Althea dropped her arms, and her eyes frantically followed the kids as they pulled a candle and an incense holder out of a plastic bag.

Scout dragged a small side table over to Pekin. She set the candle on the table carefully and lit the flame. Amber prepared the incense and lit the fragrant herbs, releasing a healing smoke that permeated the space.

"Doesn't that smell good, Althea?" Amber asked. "The candle is going to clear your negative energy from the store, and the incense will suck that nasty energy right out of you."

Mattie won't let you do this to me, she whined. *When he comes back——*

"Which won't be anytime soon. He needs to regain his

strength," Scout said. "The strength you've been siphoning off him."

"So, anyway," Pekin said. "Our plan is to make you so miserable you can't wait to leave."

Pekin pulled another handful of the obsidian and onyx crystals out of the bag and arranged them neatly on the little table around the candle and the incense. She stood back and admired her handiwork.

"I'd think you'd want to cross over," Amber said. "I mean, don't you want to see all your lost loved ones again? I bet they're all waiting for you over there, wondering what's taking you so long."

Well, you'd be wrong. I'm just fine right here.

"Unfortunately, you're not just fine right here," Pekin said. "And it's all your fault. Your son was willing, despite some reservations, to make a go of it, but you went and ruined it."

What am I supposed to do all day? It's boring!

"What did you expect?" Pekin asked. "You're *dead*, Althea! You're not supposed to be entertained all the time. You're like a steamroller running over everyone and everything to make yourself happy."

Well, I don't feel any different. You can burn all the smoke you want . . . you can even spray holy water on me . . . it's not going to make me go. Althea crossed her arms with a humph and turned her back on the teen. She started to hum. Hm hm hm hmm hmm hmm hmm. Then she added words at the top of her voice: *Ba Ba Ba Ba Ba Ber Annnn. Ta ake my haaand . . .*

Amber covered her ears and scrunched up her face. "That's awful!"

"Stop it, Althea!" Pekin yelled over the loud singing. "You're mangling that Beach Boys song!"

The ghost turned up the volume until all three kids had their hands on their ears.

Althea paused long enough to say, *I can keep this up allll day. And all night, too. Any requests?* She burst out in ghostly laughter that rattled dishes sitting on shelves all over the shop.

And then she was back to singing at the top of her lungs.

"We'll see if you're still singing the same tune after you've been bombarded by positive energy and healing vapors all night," Pekin said.

She picked up her bag and motioned to her friends. "Let's get out of here."

The haunting strains of "Barbara Ann" followed them to the front of the store and out the door.

"I *hate* her," Amber grumbled.

"You shouldn't hate her," Scout said. "But feel free to strongly dislike her." He high-fived Pekin. "I know I do."

"I'm afraid Matt might come back while we're gone," Pekin said. "He's under his mom's control."

"Yeah, I'm concerned about that too," Scout said.

"Does that mean we're leaving?" Amber asked.

Scout's mouth tightened in a thin line. "We told Matt we'd keep his mother company. I'll give you guys a ride home if you want, but I'm going to stay."

"We're all in this together," Pekin said. "But can we at

least stay out here so her stupid singing doesn't drive us all nuts?"

"Definitely. Let's just hang out until five or so," Scout said, plopping down on one of the benches in front of the shop.

"What if customers show up?" Amber asked. "Should we let them in?"

"I don't know anything about making sales or collecting money," Pekin said.

Scout shrugged. "I worked in my uncle's hardware store for a couple of summers. Maybe no one will show up, but if they do, I'll take care of it."

Luckily, no customers showed up, but, around four thirty, Matt pulled his car in behind Scout's Corolla and parked.

"What's he doing back here?" Pekin asked.

"This is what we were afraid of," Scout said. "His mother's pull is too strong. We can't let him go in there."

"I'm not sure how we can stop him," Pekin whispered behind her hand.

Scout stepped forward to meet Matt as he came up the path. "What are you doing back here?" he asked.

"I thought I should check on Mother," their client responded.

"She's fine," Scout said. "She's singing her heart out." He put a hand on Matt's arm. "I don't think you should go in there."

Matt frowned and started to push past Scout. "You can't stop me. I *hired* you, remember?"

"Of course we remember," Pekin said. "That's why we don't think you should go in there. Your mother is messing with your head. Look at you. You're not exactly the picture of health." She waved her hand over him. "I mean, really. You're thin and pale and you look kind of grayish. You can't go in there."

"But——"

"No buts," Scout said. "We're on your side. You hired us to get rid of your ghost, and by hanging around her you're making her stronger. She wants to steal all your energy. Your life force. Don't let her!"

A stronger Matt Cooley might have put up more of a fight, but this diminished Matt Cooley's shoulders slumped with a look of defeat on his face, and he stopped where he was. "Okay," he said weakly.

Pekin motioned him over to one of the benches and helped ease him onto it.

"What do I do?" Matt asked as he looked up at the three Ghosties looking down at him.

"*You* don't do anything but stay away from here," Scout said. "Leave it to us. One way or another we're going to get your mother to move on."

"I don't know if I can," Matt admitted. "I don't know if I can fight her. It's like she takes over my brain or something and tells me what to do."

"Oh my God," Amber said, putting a hand to her mouth in alarm. Her eyes were fearful as she looked at Scout.

He put a reassuring arm across her shoulder and squeezed. "Don't worry, Amber. We got this."

"Matt," Pekin said, "it will only get worse if you go near her. Look how much she's able to control you in only a couple of days. You don't have many days to go before there's nothing left of you. Maybe she'll even move into your body. You need to go back home and let us take care of this."

"Or, better yet," Scout said, "take a vacation. The more distance there is between you and your mother, the less she'll be able to control you."

"But what if I can't?" Matt asked, his brows scrunching up in misery.

"If I need to come live at your house and keep you from coming back here," Scout said, "then that's what I'll do. But you need to start taking back control. In fact, do you think you can go back in there with us and tell your mother she has to leave? If you can do that, it will make it easier for us to ease her out."

"We'll be right beside you," Pekin added. "If it looks like you can't handle it, we'll get you out of there."

Matt pursed his lips, looking doubtful.

"Your mom was making you miserable. You really don't want her here. You *know* that. Now, will you help us?"

Before he could answer, Pekin said, "Do you still have those crystals I gave you?"

Matt looked blank for a moment but then shook his head. "Not on me. I left them in the pocket of my other jacket."

"Oh, great." She frowned, then reached in the pocket of

her jeans and pulled out a few more stones and handed them to Matt. "These should help you face your mother," she said.

Everyone was nervous as Scout opened the shop door and ushered them in. The kids surrounded Matt, and they moved as one toward the salt circle.

When Althea heard the tinkle of the bell above the front door, she started singing again at the top of her lungs.

"What's that smell?" Matt asked, wrinkling his nose. "It's sort of overpowering."

"That's incense to help reduce your mother's negative energy," Pekin said. "We're burning candles too. It's all good."

"We're using all the tools we can to get the upper hand with her," Scout said.

The moment Althea spotted her son, she said, *Mattie! You came back for me. Tell these strangers to leave us alone.*

Matt looked to the Ghosties for courage and opened his mouth to speak to his mother. Then he closed his mouth and tried to turn away from her, but Scout put a hand on his shoulder and looked him in the eyes.

"You can do this, Matt. Don't chicken out." Scout squeezed his shoulder and turned him back to face the ghost.

Looking down, hand grasping the crystals in his pocket, Matt took a deep breath and said, "Mother, you are no longer welcome here. I want you to leave now."

"You heard him," Pekin said. "You are not welcome here."

Mattie, take that back. You don't mean it. You need me.

"Don't let her trick you," Pekin said. "We've got your back."

Despite the skeptical look on his face, Matt took a deep breath and said, "I mean it, Mom. I want you to go and not come back."

I'll get you for this, Mattie! I'm not going anywhere!

Matt's shoulders hunched in fear. He seemed to shrink before their eyes.

Scout grabbed his arm and started pulling him away from Althea. He felt Matt pause. "Come on, Matt," Scout urged. "You need to get out of here." He pulled more forcefully on Matt's arm.

Matt started moving, but slowly, and Scout again said urgently, "You need to get out of here," and rushed the two of them out of the store.

Mattieeee! Althea shrieked. *You won't get away with this*, she spat at Pekin.

"He wants you gone," she responded. "Let's see what a few days with the sage and the incense and the white candle do to your resolve."

Mattie will come back for me, Althea said.

"We're sending Matt away on a long vacation," Pekin said. "You won't be able to manipulate him anymore. It'll just be you and the wonderful aromas we're going to make sure are a constant part of your existence. Until you decide to cross over. All it will take is for you to agree to go into the light."

I can wait for Mattie to come back, Althea said stubbornly.

"You *can*, but we have something else in mind. Right now, we have more influence over him than you do."

What else do you have in mind? the ghost asked suspiciously.

"I guess you'll just have to wait and be surprised," Pekin said with more confidence than she felt.

"Oh," she added, "we brought earplugs in case you think continuing to sing will cause us to chicken out. So, please, entertain yourself."

Pekin nodded at Amber, and the two of them wandered back to the front of the store. She perched on the tall stool behind the counter while Amber leaned on her elbows on the counter. They could hear the ghost muttering but not loudly enough to make what she was saying clear. And, thankfully, Althea didn't start warbling "Barbara Ann" again.

"It's gonna be a long afternoon," Amber said, hanging her head.

Scout popped back inside. "Matt's on his way home and won't be back today." He crossed his fingers.

"I hope you're right," Pekin said, crossing her fingers too.

"Althea's not singing," Scout noted in surprise.

"That's because Pekin told her we had earplugs so she could sing her lungs out."

"Yeah," Pekin added. "I think it took all the fun out of it for her."

"*Do* you have earplugs?" Scout asked.

"Nah. I was bluffing. So far, it's working."

"We should be in good shape today, but I'm not sure

what tomorrow will bring," Scout said. "Or what we'll do if he tries to come back here."

"We think you should convince him to take a long vacation," Amber said. "That way, Althea can't influence him, and maybe he'll get back to normal."

"This has been our hardest job ever," Pekin said. "I hope we don't ever have another ghost like Althea to deal with."

CHAPTER NINETEEN

A MBER WAS RIGHT. It *was* a long afternoon. At the end of the day, the Ghosties filed back to the piano area to check up on Althea. Pekin had suggested they all pretend to take earplugs out so that they could continue the bluff.

There was no sign of the ghost. Could they dare to hope that their efforts had been successful?

Alas. It was not to be.

You! the ghost roared. *Bring my Mattie back.* The wind she whipped up sent more sheets of piano music fluttering through the air. Althea stomped her foot, closed her eyes, and scrunched her face up so much Pekin worried she might explode.

"Aren't you past the terrible twos tantrum stage?" Pekin asked, hands on hips. "Really, Althea. Get a grip."

"Hey," Amber asked. "Doesn't Althea look *less?*"

"Hmm?" Pekin said, tilting her head to look at the ghost. "Maybe you're right. She *does* look less."

What? What do you mean? What is less?

"I mean," Pekin said. "You're starting to fade. Without

your son here for you to steal his energy, you might just wink out of existence."

That's . . . that's preposterous, the ghost sputtered. *I feel fine.*

"Are you *sure*, Althea?" Pekin asked with a grin. "Look, Scout. Doesn't she look less . . . less . . . here?"

"I think she does," he said. "Even just since this morning. I don't think it will take long."

You're just awful children, Althea whined.

"Um, Althea," Scout responded. "We're not children. Get used to it."

"We'll just leave you here," Pekin said. "Don't worry. We'll be back in the morning. To see if there's any of you left."

Pekin laughed over her shoulder as she blew out the white candle and doused the incense. "We'll leave these here for the night," she said. "So we can get right back to making your so-called life miserable tomorrow."

How can you be so mean? Althea moaned.

"How can *you*?" Amber asked. "You're a terrible mother, trying to harm your son like that."

I was a wonderful mother. I sacrificed for that boy. He's so unappreciative.

"I'd be unappreciative too," Scout said, "if I had a mom who wanted to drain all my energy away to make herself stronger."

I hate you! I hate you all!

"We don't hate *you*, Althea," Pekin said. "We just want you to cross over. And we'll be right here to help you do it. Wanna go now?"

No! the ghost shrieked. *You can't make me. I'm not leaving my son.*

"We'll make sure your son leaves you, then," Scout said. "Did you notice we already got him to tell you to leave? If he's weak enough for you to manipulate him, he's susceptible to our *suggestions* as well. We don't do manipulation."

"It would be such a gift to your son, such a comfort, to know that his beloved mother had gone up to heaven," Pekin said. "Come on, Althea? What do you say?"

I say get out of my shop!

"Gladly," Amber said. "You're not the most fun to be around."

CHAPTER TWENTY

ONE OF THEM WERE excited to return to the antique shop; a feeling of dread and despair hung in the air. When Scout picked them up, he suggested stopping for breakfast before they faced whatever the situation waiting for them would be.

Glumly, they hunched over pancakes and scrambled eggs and orange juice.

"It's so weird, you guys," Pekin finally said. "We weren't this depressed when we left last night. What's wrong with us?"

Scout shrugged and said, "It feels like this job will go on forever. Althea's so . . . mighty. What if she wins in the end?"

"Scary thought," Pekin said. "But I know what you mean. She *is* intimidating. We have to believe in *us*, though. I think we can do this." She gazed across the table at the cheery family sitting in the booth next to them. *They* didn't have to worry about ghosts who could suck the energy right out of you.

Her thoughts couldn't help going back to those uncomplicated days before she'd wrangled her best friends into going into the ghost-busting business with her. What had she been thinking?

"Are you sorry?" she asked them. "That I got you into all this . . . mess?"

"No," Scout said immediately. "This has been the most interesting, exciting summer I've ever had." He looked at Pekin with a teasing glint in his eye. "And, if it hadn't been for what happened at Elmwood Manor, you and I might still be ignoring our feelings for each other."

"I'm not sorry either," Amber said. "Despite Althea, I agree with Scout. It's been an exciting summer."

Pekin's eyes welled with tears, and she dabbed at them with her napkin. "Thank you. I was worried about what I'd gotten you into."

"Don't feel bad about us," Scout said, squeezing her hand. "We're with you all the way."

Amber raised her water glass in a toast. "To us," she said. Three glasses clinked with a cheery sound, and they all laughed to break the tension.

The Ghosties left their breakfasts half-eaten before stepping out into the sunny August day. For *normal* people, it was probably a day for doing normal things. No one would suspect that the three teens climbing into the white Corolla with a slightly dented front bumper were on their way to face down a dead person who wouldn't move on.

There was no playful banter on the drive to Matt's store. Pekin watched through the window as the houses and fields passed by.

When Scout parked in front of the shop, Pekin tried on

a supportive smile. "Althea's had all night to stew over how she's going to deal with us. She's probably as worried as we are."

Amber paused by the front door, patting the head of one of the cast-iron Great Danes. "I remember when we first saw these dogs," she said.

"Yeah, like a week ago," Pekin said. "But I remember that you're in love with them."

"I can't help it if it's nicer out here than it is in there," Amber responded.

"Let's go face the dragon," Scout said, pulling open the front door of the shop.

"I wish you wouldn't put it like that," Amber said.

Something was wrong. It was obvious the moment the kids stepped inside. Before the door had even closed, they were bombarded by loud, scary laughter. As one, they rushed toward the piano and stopped dead in their tracks, mouths hanging open.

The salt circle had been broken and Matt sat slumped over on the piano bench.

Scout grabbed Matt's shoulder and gave it a shake. Slowly, Matt raised his head, and Scout knelt to look into his eyes.

"Son of a——," he started to say but shook his head. "No no no."

Pekin peered over Scout's shoulder at Matt and straightened back up, rubbing her face with her hand. "His eyes . . . is he even in there anymore?"

Matt's eyes were glassy and remote. He didn't respond to the Ghosties.

"We have to get him out of here," Scout said, urgency running his words together. He slung Matt's arm over his shoulders, and Pekin took Matt's other side. Amber ran ahead to open the door and stood aside as Scout and Pekin half carried Matt out of the building. They gently slid him to the porch step, and Scout peered into Matt's eyes again.

"Here, try this," Pekin said, pulling a bottle of water out of her backpack and handing it to Scout.

At first, the water dribbled out of Matt's mouth, and then he sputtered, and his eyes cleared.

"I feel like hell," he said, rubbing the back of his head.

"What happened in there?" Scout asked him. "What happened to the salt circle?"

Matt looked at the ground and didn't answer right away. "I couldn't help it," he mumbled. "I needed to check on her and the . . . I don't know what happened."

"We're doing our best here, Matt," Scout said. "We're about ready to leave you to figure this out on your own. I don't know what else we can do for you."

Matt reached up and grabbed Scout's T-shirt. "Please. I'm not strong enough to fight her. I *need* you."

Scout and his friends sank down on the porch steps, no one speaking. The now-revived Matt looked from one of them to another and, after what sounded like a sob, choked out, "Please."

"You keep trying to undermine us," Amber said. "We thought we were finally getting somewhere. Your mother was trapped in a small space. We had these tools, and we were going to wear her down. Then you come here . . .

after we told you how important it was for you to stay away . . . and you let her out of the circle. Why would we even try anymore?"

"But if you help me, maybe I can be strong," Matt pleaded.

"Do we have to move in with you and put a lock on your door?"

"*I* don't know," he whined. He was already less pale, and his eyes didn't have the frightened look he'd had only a few minutes earlier. He was becoming more substantial by the minute, the weakness caused by his mother's influence fading away.

"How could she reach him when he was at home?" Amber asked.

"I'm not sure," Pekin said, "but I think they're connected somehow because of how much she's been able to absorb his energy. That's all I can think of."

"It makes sense," Scout said. "Since she couldn't leave the shop. But she's familiar with his home, so maybe, if she concentrated, she would be able to touch his mind."

He motioned for Pekin and Amber to step away from Matt so they could discuss their options. The most obvious plan was to have Matt out of the picture completely.

Rejoining Matt, Scout crossed his arms and stared down his client. "You have one more chance with us. Here's what we need you to do. Leave town."

Matt sputtered. "What? I can't go. I have a business to run."

"It's your choice, but we won't help you unless you take a long vacation."

"But, my business——"

"Put a sign on the door," Pekin said. "People with businesses take vacations all the time. If you're anywhere near, your mother can siphon off your energy and grow stronger. She'll be stronger and you . . . won't be."

"It may already be too late," Scout said. "She thinks she's in control now. We're willing to go back in there and go all out to get rid of her, but only if you agree to leave town until we say the coast is clear." Scout put his hands on his hips. "So, what's it gonna be?"

Matt stared back silently, then stood and paced up and down the sidewalk in front of his shop while the teens watched. He marched back and opened his mouth to speak, then closed his mouth and went back down to the sidewalk and resumed pacing.

The Ghosties shared a look, not sure whether they hoped he'd agree or not. None of them would mind turning the keys back over to Matt and letting him deal with his own mother.

When he finally joined them again, Matt agreed to stay away. Far away.

"We'll know if you come back here," Pekin said. "We have our ways."

"Yeah," Scout added. "And if you *do* come back, we're out of here."

"Okay, okay," Matt said tightly. "Can I go in there and make up a sign?"

"No," Pekin said. "Tell us what you need and we'll go get it."

Inside the front counter was a preprinted sign with blanks for dates and times. Once Pekin had retrieved it, Matt indicated the shop would be closed for the next two weeks. Sheepishly, he shook hands with each of the kids, promised to give them his itinerary, and climbed into his SUV and drove away.

Pekin drew in a breath and slowly blew it out as Scout ushered them back into the eerily silent shop. They immediately felt a chill in the air.

"Uh-oh," Amber said.

"I know," Pekin said. "I think she's up to something."

"Let's split up and see if we can find her," Scout said, and the three of them headed for different areas of the shop.

Before they separated, Pekin handed each of them a crystal for whatever protection the stones could provide against the ghost of Althea Cooley.

Despite the chill, nothing seemed out of place, and no ghostly voice addressed them. None of the kids felt reassured by this, however, knowing Althea was toying with them.

After his search of the shop turned up no sign of the ghost, Scout said loudly, "You might as well come out, Althea. Matt's gone and he's not coming back. You have to deal with us now."

Oh, I'm sooo scared, the ghost responded.

Ignoring the voice, Pekin continued her sweep of the shop, sticking her head into the supply room. When she turned back toward the interior, she heard an odd swishing sound, and from around a corner marched half-a-dozen dolls with painted porcelain faces and frilly party dresses, each about two feet tall.

Her hand flew to her mouth in alarm, and she called out for her friends. In an instant, Scout was at her side with Amber close behind. They all stared in wide-eyed shock at the approaching doll army, and Althea's laughter boomed around them.

The dolls formed themselves into a semicircle around the kids, cutting off any escape route. Scout motioned Pekin and Amber into the supply room and turned back to face the scary toys. Glancing over his shoulder at the girls with an encouraging smile, looking braver than he felt, he squared his shoulders and planted his feet, ready to meet the silent troop. For a moment, it appeared they were in a standoff until the dolls' eyes started blinking and their jaws clacked open and closed exposing teeth that were pointed and menacing, definitely not innocent doll teeth. And they were going *num num num num*. Pekin shrieked and clutched Amber's arm as the dolls moved toward them, still going *num num num num.*

"What *are* they?" Amber whined, covering her ears and huddling against Pekin.

His back to Pekin and Amber, Scout spread his arms out to protect them. One of the dolls rushed forward, an odd, tinny battle cry emanating from it. Both girls screamed as the doll surged toward Scout and flew into the air in front of him, its arms reaching for his face. Scout raised his hands instinctively and batted it away. The doll fell in a heap on the floor in a cloud of taffeta and ribbons. He was speechless for a moment, and suddenly he laughed. "Really, Althea? Dolls?"

He grabbed the creepy toy closest to him and one by one smashed them on the floor. Shattered doll heads and arms and legs flew everywhere, and Althea screamed in rage. Scout stomped on an errant doll eye that rolled around on the floor. "What else you got, Ghost?"

Just you wait, you awful kids. You'll find out.

"Well, you better come up with something soon. Your energy is going to start leaking away now that Matt's not here."

He'll come back for me. He loves me.

"I wouldn't count on it," Pekin said. "Your son is about to take a long vacation. You won't be able to entice him to come back. You won't be able to find him. But, don't worry, we'll be here."

"Right," Amber said. "And we're not sharing our energy with you."

At that, wind swirled through the shop, and the sound of breaking glass lasted for several seconds.

"I'm hungry," Scout said. "Want to order a pizza?"

His boldness surprised Pekin and Amber, who were still processing the brazen way he'd taken on the scary dolls. "Sounds good to me," Pekin gulped out.

"What do you like on your pizza, Althea?" Scout asked with a smirk. "Oh. That's right. You can't eat pizza anymore."

A painting flew off the wall and knocked a china pitcher and bowl set off a mahogany sideboard.

"Now, now, Althea," Scout said, grinning wickedly. "You're a little old for tantrums, aren't you?"

Get out! Get out! Get out! The ghost materialized in front of them, her whole body heaving from her struggle to catch her breath. She clenched and unclenched her hands.

I'll make you pay! She seemed to pulse with rage.

Pekin and Amber looked to Scout, neither feeling as brave as he seemed to be.

At a wave of the ghost's hand, an old oval mirror, streaked and dusty, smashed into jagged pieces on the floor. Slivers of glass flew toward the teens, who only through luck missed being cut by the shards.

Pekin straightened her shoulders. "Althea, knock it off. We have to talk."

Scout tilted his head, pursed his lips, and nodded in appreciation of his girlfriend's grit. "Way to go, Pekie!"

"I mean it, Althea. We'll bring holy water with us next time. It gets rid of demons so you ought to be a piece of cake. We can make you miserable. Don't think we won't."

Amber glanced back and forth between Scout and Pekin, mouthing "holy water?" There was no doubt Amber wasn't keen on stealing holy water again.

"It's a bluff," Scout whispered behind his hand. "But Althea doesn't know that."

"Yeah," Amber puffed up her courage. "Maybe it'll make you melt. Like the Wicked Witch in *The Wizard of Oz*."

"Good one, Amber," Scout said with a grin and a high-five.

I hate you, the ghost grumbled, anger almost causing the air around her to ripple.

"Don't you get tired of wearing that same old ratty pink jogging suit all the time?" Pekin asked. "I mean, it wouldn't be something *I'd* choose to go through eternity in."

"Me neither," Amber added. "You can probably wear whatever you want after you cross over."

More dishes clattered to the ground, and Scout had to duck when a china teacup whizzed by his head.

"Just for that," Pekin said, "we're getting our friend, who happens to be a professional medium, to come here, and we're going to do a séance to banish you from this store."

You're the meanest people on earth! Althea started to cry, loud sobs shaking her pink-clad body.

"Look who's talking," Amber said. "You were trying to destroy your own son."

"We're through talking to you," Pekin said. "We're going to go order our pizza and sit outside. Go ahead and break things in here. If you don't care anything about your very own shop, we don't either."

The ghost shrieked in anger and rushed at Pekin, grabbing fistfuls of her hair and yanking.

Pekin screamed, but her friends couldn't break Althea's grip.

"What do we do?" Amber's face reflected her horror.

Scout wrapped his arms around Pekin and, with Amber's help, pulled her toward the front of the store. Althea let go of Pekin's hair, but her hands clasped around Pekin's throat, and she started squeezing. Pekin gasped for air.

"Stop!" Amber screamed at Althea and tried to pull her off of Pekin, but her hands went right through the ghost. Althea's face turned toward Amber, and that momentary lack of attention allowed Scout to reach the front door, shouting at Amber to open it.

Althea growled and tried to regain her grip on Pekin's neck, but, with a final surge of strength, Scout and Amber hustled Pekin out the front door, and the ghost's hands disappeared at the threshold.

Scout pulled Pekin into an embrace, his arms tightening around her as she trembled and then collapsed against him. "What do I do?" he asked Amber, his voice shaking.

"Sit her down here." She indicated one of the benches. "Should I call 911?"

"Yes!" he shouted, but, before he could lower Pekin onto the bench, she stiffened in his arms and looked around in bewilderment.

"What happened?" she asked.

"Althea attacked you," he said. "Amber's going to call 911."

"No. Don't do that," she said weakly. "I'm all right." She rubbed her neck, where red welts were already beginning to appear. She shivered as Scout let go of her so she could sit down. "I'm so cold."

"Probably from Althea touching you. Are you sure you're all right?" he asked, sitting down and slipping his arms around her. "Maybe we should take you to the ER just in case."

Pekin rolled her head and then her shoulders. "No. We can't do that. I think I'm okay. Besides, if I go to the hospital, my parents will find out, and they might not let me come back here."

"And maybe they'd be right," Scout said, standing. "Pekie, I was scared I was going to lose you. Again."

"I'm really okay, Scout." She teared up at his concern. "I'm sorry it scared you, but I'm stronger than you give me credit for." She stood and touched his cheek, kissing him lightly, as her eyes welled with tears.

"It was that awful Althea," Amber said, throwing her arms around Pekin and Scout. "I'm so glad you're okay."

"I'm kinda scared to go back in there," Amber said.

"I'm wondering whether we should too," Scout added.

"We can't abandon Matt," Pekin insisted. "But maybe we should ask Mildew what to do."

"I'm all for that," Scout said. "We may be in over our heads."

"Can we just put the 'Closed' sign on the door and go home?" Amber asked, her eyes big with worry.

"I guess," Pekin said. "I've had all the Althea I can stand today."

"I'm glad you're on board with that suggestion," Scout said and frowned. "Pekie. Your neck! There are finger marks. Red ones. Your mom is gonna freak when she sees them."

Pekin carefully felt her neck. "It's kinda sore. Can we stop at the mall on the way home so I can buy a scarf or something?"

"No. Turtlenecks," Amber said. "Sleeveless ones are the latest in summer fashion."

"Sure they are," the always practical Scout said, rolling his eyes.

"Well, they *could* be," Amber retorted.

"I think we should stop by Mildew's before we go to the mall," Scout said. "She needs to see what happened to you."

Despite their forced bravado, the kids knew they were just whistling past the graveyard.

CHapter Twenty-One

~~~~~~

T
HE GHOSTIES DIDN'T TELL Mildew they were coming, but the diminutive medium didn't seem surprised when she opened the door. One of the perks of being psychic.

She greeted them with a warm smile, which faltered when she spotted Pekin's neck.

"We ran into a little problem," Scout said.

"Does it have something to do with that?" Mildew asked, indicating Pekin.

"Yes," Amber said. "Althea tried to kill Pekin. We were lucky to get her out of there."

"Tell me everything." Mildew's forehead furrowed as she ushered the teens into her family room. "I'll be right back," she added.

It was a relief to be somewhere they felt safe after the haunted shop. Their faces lit up when Mildew returned bearing a tray with ice water, sodas, and cookies.

"Are you all right, Pekin?" she asked.

"Now I am," Pekin said. "I didn't know she'd turn evil like that, though."

"I don't know what we should do," Amber squeaked. "Althea is *really* strong."

"We've threatened her with holy water and séances," Pekin said. "She seems worried about a séance."

"Yeah. But why should she be?" Amber asked. "Séances aren't for banishing ghosts. Doesn't she know that?"

"Maybe not," Mildew said. "Ghosts don't 'hang out' like living people do. It's not as if she has ghost friends filling her in on everything. Ghosts learn things as they go about their hauntings. Trial and error."

"What should we do?" Amber asked. "Can you go back with us? And what happens if she attacks again? We couldn't do anything to stop her. Not really."

"Of course I will," Mildew said. "I'm thinking we go in armed with all our tools. Or weapons. if you prefer. If, and this is only an *if*, she attacks any of us, we'll know right where she is and can throw a quick salt circle around her while she's focused on the victim of her attack. If that happens, we can throw more salt right on her to distract her and help the person she's attacking get away. The smaller the area we can contain her in, the less attractive remaining there will be for her."

"But she'll still be in the shop," Pekin said.

"I have an idea about that. Assuming we can trap her in a salt circle, we'll tell her we've convinced Mr. Cooley to close the shop and open a new one somewhere else. And, if we add that he's not going to sell the shop so she'll have no one else's energy to drain, she might be willing to cross over."

"It's worth a shot," Scout said. "But I think Pekin shouldn't be there because she's already been attacked."

Mildew looked at Pekin, one eyebrow raised. "That may be a good idea."

"No, it's not a good idea," Pekin said with a huff. "I'm not going to let that . . . that . . . *ghost* win. Besides, she could have attacked any of us. It's not like she targeted me because I'm weak or anything ridiculous like that. I'll be fine with all of you there. Just keep the salt handy."

"But, Pekie—"

"Sorry, Scout. But I want to be there. You'll keep me safe. I know it." She leaned against his shoulder, and he slung his arm around her and rested his head on hers for a moment before holding her away so he could make sure she was paying attention.

"Pekie, she tried to kill you. Like, an *hour* ago," he said heatedly. "You can't put yourself in that position again."

"We don't know what might set her off. I can't promise it won't be me. And that's all I'll say about that."

Scout clenched his teeth. "I give up. Nobody can talk you out of anything."

Pekin grinned. "Yep."

"We're waiting until tomorrow, though," Scout said. "I'm not ready for another round with Althea today."

Pekin looked at Mildew. "Are you available tomorrow?"

"Of course. And don't worry. We'll figure this out."

Pekin's shoulders slumped. "I don't know. I feel like we've failed. I was so sure we could deal with any situation that came along, but, so far, we've let Matt down. Maybe we should just give up."

"Pekie," Scout said. "A few minutes ago you said you weren't going to let that ghost win. You know you don't want to quit."

She sighed heavily. "You're right, of course. I was just feeling a little wave of despair for a minute there."

"Sometimes," Amber asked meekly, "*does* the ghost win?"

No one said anything as they looked to Mildew for reassurance.

"That *is* a possibility, but we're going to do our best not to let that happen."

Chapter Twenty-Two

S HOPPING FOR A HIGH-NECKED top wasn't as quick or easy as the girls thought it would be. Turns out, sleeveless turtlenecks weren't so popular after all. Pekin glanced sympathetically at Scout, telling him he could go check out the watch department or something else he found more interesting, and she'd text him when they were ready to go. Finally, on a sale rack at the big department store anchoring one end of the mall, they struck gold. Pekin grabbed four of them. "Problem solved."

THE NEXT MORNING, MILDEW met the kids at the antique shop, commenting on how nice Pekin looked in her new coral turtleneck. Pekin smiled and unlocked the front door.

Before they went in, Scout said, "You're not thinking of hosting a ghost, are you?"

"Of course not! It's your turn to host a ghost, remember?" Amber said with a wicked grin. "Pekin and I have already done it."

Pekin laughed weakly. "I don't think we need to host

this one. We can't get her to shut up." She felt a little guilty at the concern on Scout's face.

"Mildew wouldn't let her anyway," Amber said.

"Shall we?" Pekin asked, opening the door.

Greeting them when they entered were three ghastly watercolor paintings sitting on little easels atop the counter, a portrait of each of the Ghosties. Pekin gasped when she saw them. In the painting of her, Pekin was posed scarecrow-like with her head hanging at an odd angle, her eyes missing.

In Scout's picture, he stood with slumped shoulders, looking up through rivers of blood coursing down his face.

And for Amber, it was as if the ghost had plumbed her deepest fears. Her painted hands clasped her face as large spiders crawled all over her. Her mouth was open in a scream, her eyes wide in terror, her hair flying up from her head like static electricity surrounded her.

"What *are* those?" Pekin whispered, backing into Scout. She reached out for her portrait, but Mildew put a hand on her arm to stop her.

"Not a good idea," the little medium said.

Tears filled a frightened Amber's eyes, and Mildew hurriedly ushered the kids back out the door. "Don't let Althea see you cry," she admonished once they were outside.

"But those pictures——" Amber choked out.

"Those pictures are the ghost's attempt to scare you away. You can't let her. The three of you march back inside like the warriors you are."

No one moved.

"Althea is sick," Scout growled through clenched teeth.

"Yes, she is." Mildew confirmed, gently squeezing his arm.

"Go on, Pekin," Mildew said. "You know what to do."

She grimaced and clenched her fists. Gathering her courage, she squared her shoulders and lifted her head, determination reflected in her eyes. "Let's go."

Swinging open the front door, Pekin stepped inside. The little bell over the front door tinkled loudly. Feet planted, she said loudly, "Really, Althea? First dolls and now paintings?"

She swept her arm across the counter, sending the three paintings toppling to the floor. "This is what we think of your artistic abilities, Althea," she said as she stomped on each of the paintings and kicked them out the door. "*That's* what we think of your clown pictures."

Amber's mouth was hanging open as she watched her brave friend.

"Way to go, Pekie!"

"We're tired of your little games, Althea," Pekin said. "It's time for you to leave."

A pink blob morphed into Althea in her tracksuit. *You ungrateful fools. I* slaved *over those watercolors. Ah, well, I can do more.*

The ghost posed with shoulders thrown back and chest thrust forward, and she raised one hand to pat her orangey hair, turning her head as if basking in the Ghosties' admiration.

What's wrong with your neck, dearie? the ghost addressed

Pekin. *Did you hurt yourself? Oh, wait . . . I did that, didn't I?* Ghostly laughter filled the shop.

"We're here to set up for the séance we're going to perform to get you out of here," Pekin said, pulling the neck of her turtleneck higher.

"Yes, we are," Amber added in her bravest voice. She held up a handful of crystals. "And we brought backup."

Althea wavered for a moment but quickly returned to sashaying around in front of her audience. *You can't hurt me.*

"We're not trying to hurt you," Mildew said, stepping forward. "We're going to make sure you move on. In the natural progression of life, you belong on the other side of the divide between life and death."

What if I'm not ready to move on?

"We plan to convince you otherwise," Mildew said.

"You don't want us to do a séance on your . . . rear end," Amber said.

"Nice," Mildew nodded at Amber. "I'm glad you cleaned that up."

"Well, I don't like to swear," she replied.

"I'm proud of you, dear."

Althea, hands on hips, glared at Mildew. *Who are you anyway?*

"Your worst nightmare," Mildew said, grinning wickedly.

Aww, the kiddies need their mother to come save their little behinds. Aren't you the cutest little cowards.

"We're not cowards, Althea," Scout said. "But we're smart enough to bring in help when we need it. Our gain. Your loss."

Mildew put her hands on her hips. "Let's get set up. We'll need a table, round if possible, and four chairs. Scout, can you see what you can find for us?"

"Althea, you can save us some time," Scout said. "Where should I look for the table and chairs?"

A cold wind swept through the shop, rattling dishes, and Althea shook her fist. *Get out of my shop!*

Ignoring her, Scout set off down one of the aisles, and in a moment he was back. "I found a round dining set we can use back there." He turned, and the others followed him.

Mildew arranged three white candles on the table and put a dark crystal at each seat. Scout arranged the chairs for everyone and took a seat.

"Where is she?" Pekin asked as she sat down.

"Is a ghost technically a she or an it?" Scout asked. "I'm not sure."

How dare you? Althea shrieked, bursting into view in the aisle beside the table. *I'm a she! I'm not an it!*

"We're just not sure about that," Pekin said, standing and advancing toward the ghost. "I mean, *technically*, you're no longer a person. So, *voilà!* You're an it!"

The ghost lunged at Pekin and grabbed her around the neck. Again.

Momentarily stunned, Amber and Scout watched, mouths open, until Mildew yelled, "Grab the salt!"

She was already circling the struggling pair with her box of salt, and Scout quickly jumped in to complete the circle. Pekin was flailing around, unable to dislodge the rage-filled ghost.

"Help her!" Amber yelled.

The ghost had been too intent on murdering Pekin to notice the salt caper and still didn't turn her attention away from Pekin until Mildew threw a handful of salt directly on her.

Althea shrieked, and her hands dropped as she whipped around, looking for the source of whatever had attacked her, which gave Scout an opening to jerk Pekin out of the circle, being careful not to disturb the salt line.

Pekin's arms flew around Scout's neck, and she held on tight, eyes squeezed shut. Mildew sent Amber to the kitchenette for a bottle of water, and Amber took off at a run.

Once assured that Pekin was all right, Scout let her go and advanced on the angry pink puff that was Althea.

"Let's see how much fun you have stuck in that tiny little circle. You can't get out. You hear me? You can't get out!"

Mattie will let me out. You'll see.

"Mattie's not coming back," Scout said.

I can wait longer than you can.

"You *could* wait, but it will be a long one. And, in the meantime, you're stuck. I mean, how much fun can you have in there?"

"I don't think you're ghostly enough," Pekin managed to choke out past her traumatized throat. "I like ghosts that disappear sometimes. Ones that hide from the living. You're *constantly* around. And, instead of having to beg for a ghost to talk to us, you're always babbling about something. I wish we couldn't see or hear you. Why don't you go to that other place ghosts go to be alone?" She rubbed her neck. "In case you can't guess, I *really* don't like you."

You're not exactly a walk in the park either, dearie, Althea snipped.

"This isn't getting us anywhere," Mildew pronounced, lighting the white candles and preparing a dish of cedar incense. "Ghosties, take a seat."

That smells disgusting, Althea said, waving her hand in front of her face to dispel the cedar aroma. Of course, not having a real hand, Althea didn't affect the smoke.

"I think it smells nice," Amber said sweetly.

Chin resting in her palm, Mildew seemed thoughtful. "You know," she mused, "I think your ghost hasn't had enough time to enjoy her aloneness. I vote we adjourn and meet again tomorrow. See how antsy she is by then."

"Can we leave the incense on?" Amber asked.

"Much as I'd love to do that," Mildew said, "I don't want to take the chance Althea accidentally knocks it over and burns down the shop."

"That *would* solve the haunting problem," Scout said drily.

"Maybe not. She might still be attached to the location."

Mildew collected her candles and crystals and motioned for Amber to bring the incense.

"You're kind of a jerk," Pekin directed at the trapped ghost. "You won't *ever* win. I promise."

Althea responded with a loud raspberry, ghost spittle flying everywhere.

"Classy, Althea," Pekin said as a parting shot.

Chapter Twenty-Three

~~~~~~

"**A**NOTHER DAY, ANOTHER fun time with Althea," Scout said to his passengers the next morning, his tone leaving no question about his lack of enthusiasm for the task. Scout, Pekin and Amber were en route to the antique shop, not the least bit excited about their upcoming encounter with a particularly nasty ghost.

"Hopefully, this will be our last fun day with Althea," Pekin said, shuddering at the thought of cold, ghostly hands around her throat and adjusting her yellow turtleneck. "I don't want a ghost to *ever* touch me again," she said. "It's creepy."

"I'm kinda scared," Amber offered. "I hate her."

"Me too," Pekin said.

"Probably about as much as she hates us," Scout said.

"Look. Mildew's already here," Pekin said, waving as they pulled into the parking lot.

"Everyone ready?" Mildew asked when they were all gathered outside the shop.

A chorus of "yes" and "let's go" met her question, and Pekin unlocked the door.

Marching directly to the séance area, followed by the Ghosties, Mildew reached into her bag and withdrew a round red tablecloth, decorated with moons and stars, and arranged the three white candles and the crystals, then set the dish with the incense on the table and lit it. Giving it a moment to kindle and begin to release its scent, she waved her hand to disperse the smoke in the direction of the salt circle, which initially appeared empty.

"Did she get out?" Amber asked, her forehead furrowed in anxiety.

"Oh no. I expect she'll be making an appearance any moment now," Mildew said.

As if summoned, Althea's pink form wavered into view, her nose wrinkled in distaste at the aroma of the incense.

"Good morning, Althea," Mildew said. "Have you decided to go away yet?"

I'm not leaving. I'm going to stay here with my son.

"Your son's not here," Pekin said.

He'll be back for me, the ghost said confidently.

"Not this time," Scout said. "We'll make sure of that."

I can wait.

"You'll be waiting all alone. Forever," Pekin said.

"We've convinced Matt to close the shop," Scout said. "He'll find another location for it, and, in case you think you can take up with the new owners where you left off with Matt, we'll make sure he doesn't sell it."

"So it'll sit here empty. And you'll be restricted to this tiny little spot. All alone."

"Forever," Amber added.

The ghost appeared to smolder, her bulk growing and shrinking as if she were breathing her rage in and out. She almost looked like she might explode.

Why don't you leave me alone? Althea wailed.

"That's the plan," Scout said. "Oh, wait. Did you mean why are we doing this to you?"

"Because we can," Amber taunted.

"What she means," Scout said, "is we won't leave you alone because you drained your son of his life force, and you tried to murder Pekin. That makes you evil. We're not going to leave you alone until you cross over to where you belong."

"We'll give you a few minutes to consider that while we prepare for the séance," Mildew said before turning to the Ghosties.

"Let's say a protection prayer before we get started."

What's with all the praying? the ghost asked scornfully.

"Sometimes in a séance, things come through we don't want to come through," Mildew said. "The prayer is to protect us from those things."

What things?

"Hopefully, nothing you need to worry about," Mildew responded. "Shall we? Let's hold hands and pray."

Althea watched curiously until Mildew ended her prayer with "Amen."

"You'll be *sooo* lonely," Amber said. "I feel sorry for you."

How dare you? Althea spit out. *You children are nothing.*

"We're more than you are," Pekin said. "We're still

alive and you're not." She turned to Mildew. "Are you ready?"

"Yes. We can start now."

I'm not afraid of your séance. It can't do anything to me. I know all about séances. They just call spirits so you can talk to them. I'm already here, so what's the point? Althea crossed her arms over her chest, trying to appear confident.

"Apparently, you get your information from the movies. You know what else a séance can do?" Mildew smiled kindly at the ghost. "It can call spirits from the other side who will *escort* you back with them. And don't think it will be pleasant."

You're bluffing, Althea said, but her posture shifted from her confident stance. She seemed suddenly unsure.

"Are we? Do you want to wait and find out?" Mildew asked. "Your crossing over will be much more pleasant if you leave on your own without being dragged across."

They all seemed at a standoff, the Ghosties knowing the séance couldn't do what Mildew was promising, and Althea not sure Mildew wasn't telling the truth.

"Everyone take hands," Mildew said, "and close your eyes."

The kids did as she directed, and Mildew started chanting softly under her breath. No one knew what she was saying, but Althea's wide-open eyes reflected her concern as she watched. Mildew chanted on, then said aloud, "Spirit come forth and take this ghost."

Nooo! Althea shrieked. *Stop. Stop right now!*

Mildew paused in her chanting when Pekin put a hand

on her arm and said, "Give me a minute. I want to say something to Althea."

She stood and faced the ghost. "The undeniable truth, Althea, is that you don't belong here anymore. You'll only be a shadow, an empty vessel, unable to engage, to participate, to be part of life that's going on around you. Without you."

Loud sobs burst from the ghost. She cried inconsolably, while Mildew and the Ghosties looked on in silence.

"Why is it so important for you to stay here?" Pekin asked, as if suddenly aware that there might be a reason for Althea's reluctance to cross over.

Because no one wants to die. To be forgotten like you were never there. I wasn't ready. I never got to see Paris!

"Did you have a trip to Paris planned?"

No. I doubt I'd have ever gone. But there were a lot of things I never did. And now I'll never get to.

"That's what happens with everyone when they die, Althea. Do you think most people are ready when their time comes? And your son won't forget you. You'll live on in the memories of people you leave behind."

Pekin felt herself softening toward the dejected ghost. "If I were to . . . to . . . die, even though I truly love my family and friends, and would be filled with grief at the thought of leaving them, I'd know that my time on earth was over. I'd look forward to what awaited me on the other side of that white light. And I'd wait, with an open heart, for the ones I love to join me when their time comes. You're stuck here, in this spot. Instead of crossing over to see what mysteries and joy await you, you'll stand in that spot. For eternity. No one else will come to set you free from this nonexistence. You only have us. If you turn us down, that's it for you."

Althea's sobs quieted to sniffles, and Pekin said in a soothing voice, "Althea, stop fighting us. You don't really want to spend eternity like this, do you? Alone and lonely?"

But what will happen to me over there?

"No one knows what awaits you on the other side," Mildew said, her voice soft. "Maybe your parents, your husband, your loved ones who passed on before you. You've kept them waiting a long time. Isn't there someone you miss and would love to see again?"

My sister Helen passed away when I was sixteen, and I've never stopped missing her.

"She could be waiting, just past the veil, to welcome you. Wouldn't that be lovely?"

But I've done bad things. What if I don't go where she is?

"But what if you do?" Mildew said. "There is forgiveness if you want it. If you ask for it. It's up to you now."

Althea didn't say anything for a long moment, chewing on her lip, smoothing down her hair, fidgeting, as the Ghosties and Mildew looked on. Then she straightened her shoulders and lifted her head stoically.

Okay. Okay. I give up. Where's that stupid light I'm supposed to see?

Everyone let out a collective sigh of relief.

"It's not a stupid light," Mildew said. "It's a gift to help you on your way."

All the fight seemed to drain out of Althea. The ghost visibly relaxed. *I'm sorry.*

"You might want to apologize to Pekin," Scout said through clenched teeth.

Althea's gaze settled on Pekin, a wry smile on the ghost's face. *I didn't mean to try to kill you. I'm sorry for that too.*

"I forgive you," Pekin said, trying hard to mean it.

Mildew waved her hand in the air. "Look, now, Althea. What do you see?"

Althea's eyes grew big as her vision seemed to clear. *It's so bright . . .*

And she was gone.

There was silence for a moment. Then Amber squeaked excitedly, "Oh, my God! Did that just happen?"

"It sure did," Mildew said with a huge smile. She blew out the candles and snuffed the incense, then began to pack up her tools.

Scout moved the table and chairs back where he'd found them and wiped his hands together. "I say we get out of here."

"That was exhausting," Pekin said. "I feel like a burger. Can we go to Benny's?"

"Would you like to join us, Mildew?" Amber asked.

"Lead the way," the little medium said with a grin that stretched ear to ear.

Chapter Twenty-Four

~~~~~~

O VER COMFORT FOOD, the four discussed the way the case ended. Pekin filled Mildew in on the way it had evolved. The sad, sweet mother who couldn't bear to be parted from her beloved son. The conflicted son who bowed to his mother's insistent pleas and agreed to let her stay. The hollow-eyed zombie the son had become as his mother sucked the energy right out of him.

The devolution of the ghost into a monster whose rage drove her to increasingly brutal attacks on the three Ghosties.

Then, inexplicably, Althea was gone. For good this time.

"Thanks for helping us, Mildew," Pekin said. "I was worried we might fail this time."

"No need to thank me. I'm proud of the way the three of you are developing your skills."

Scout nodded an acknowledgment of her words, but kept intently typing on his tablet, catching Pekin's attention.

"What are you doing?" she asked him.

"Writing everything down. For our *Spirit Investigation*

Report." He smiled at Mildew, who'd given him the idea of keeping the reports after their first case.

"Oh," Pekin said. "That's a good idea. Thanks for doing that."

"I want to say something else," Mildew said, and everyone's attention focused on her.

"The three of you handled a difficult situation very well. Scout, you got right in Althea's face and scoffed at her tricks. Amber, your lack of fear and eagerness to jump in wherever needed really stood out." Mildew clasped her hands in front of her. "Pekin . . . Pekin, how did you know to say that to Althea? It was masterful."

Pekin squirmed, embarrassed. "I tried to think about things from her point of view, about what she was hoping to achieve by staying. I was pretty sure it didn't include being trapped in a small circle all alone. I thought about what might cause me to want to give up, and I just said it."

"Whatever your inspiration was," Mildew said, "great job."

"Thanks. I'm shocked it worked. I never expected what I said would result in Althea voluntarily moving on."

"It's such a relief it's all over," Scout said, squeezing Pekin's hand. "This was a tough one."

"You should probably call Matt and tell him it's safe to come home," Pekin said.

"Yeah," Amber added. "I'm glad we didn't have to tell him he had to sell the shop."

"I know," he said. "Nice bluff."

"Can we take a break now?" Amber asked. "I want to

enjoy at least *some* of the summer while it's still left."

"I second that," Pekin said.

"We only have a few more weeks," Scout said, "and I have practice, which will take more of my time. I don't think we'll have time for this after school starts. This might be our final case."

"Now I can spend more time with Josh," Amber said, blushing. "I think he misses me."

"You all deserve a break," Mildew said. "You've solved three cases and should feel proud of yourselves."

"I might miss it, though," Pekin said, suddenly somber.

"We don't have to rule anything out," Scout said. "What will be will be."

"You sound like a mystic," Pekin laughed.

He grinned wickedly. "Maybe that'll be my next job."

"Enough talking," Mildew said. "Our burgers are getting cold."

"MATT WANTS US TO MEET him at the shop tomorrow morning," Pekin said. They were relaxing in Pekin's family room after saying goodbye to Mildew. Scout had suggested that an afternoon playing video games was just what they needed. Imaginary battles instead of ones that were all too real.

She'd stepped into the kitchen to make the call to Matt and update him before the game started. "We can give him the *Spirit Investigation Report* Scout prepared, and he can pay us the rest of our fee. Does that work for you guys?"

"Sure," Amber said.

"I can do it," Scout said. "That will be our last piece of business with him, and we can close the door on it forever." He did a little fist pump.

"How did he sound on the phone?" Amber asked.

"Relieved," Pekin said. "I was worried he'd be sad that his mother was really gone, but he's happy he can come home again."

"I'm glad he's relieved," Scout said. "I bet not nearly as relieved as we are."

"I would be if I was him," Pekin said. "Especially once I started feeling like myself again."

"Oh, um," Amber started, suddenly looking sheepish. "I forgot to tell you. Josh invited me to a party next week. You guys are invited too. The cheer squad is putting it on and—"

"Wait," Pekin sat forward. "Is it Vanessa Dooley's party?" Her face felt hot.

"Um, it is," Amber said, a little line appearing between her eyebrows. "But it'll be okay. Really. Josh says it should be super fun, and Vanessa really wants you to be there, Pekie."

"I doubt that. She wants Scout to be there. She definitely wasn't inviting me when she asked Scout to help her with the party."

"Pekin." Scout turned her to face him. "I haven't received an invitation. We don't have to go if you don't want to, but you can't be mad at me for this. It's not my fault."

Pekin looked ready to aggressively pounce but instead drew a breath. "No, Scout. I'm not mad at you. And . . . and . . . if you want to go . . . we can." She wasn't smiling though.

Her elation at the successful end of their case seemed to fade. She was quieter than usual, and the video game failed to hold her attention, even though she tried to smile and participate so her friends could enjoy playing. When it was time to go, Scout looked at her with worried eyes, as if he were not quite convinced that she was okay with the whole Vanessa thing. He kissed her goodbye.

Pekin was quiet during dinner with her parents later, answering questions but not chattering excitedly about the antique shop ghost. Considering that her mother had seen ghosts of her own when she was a girl, it was unusual for Pekin not to be exuberantly spilling all the details.

Trudging up the stairs to her room after dinner, Pekin's mood was dark. She wasn't sure she wasn't a little angry with Scout, but she couldn't really blame him. She was just uncomfortable with the idea of Scout hanging around Vanessa Dooley, even if Pekin was with him.

Pekin knew she was being unfair, but she couldn't seem to shake the anxiety that had thrown a blanket over her exhilaration of a job well done.

Wanna talk? A text from Amber.

Pekin sighed, not sure she felt like talking, even to her best friend, but she responded *okay.*

Good. I'll be over in five minutes.

A FEW MINUTES LATER, Amber stood in the doorway of Pekin's bedroom, observing her friend sulking on her bed. Amber waved her hand in a sweeping motion at Pekin and said, "This is why I came over. I knew you were upset about the party."

Pekin glared at her. "So what if I am?"

"What have you got to be upset about? It's a party. It'll be fun, or it *can* be fun if you stop sulking about it."

"But Scout——"

"That's it, isn't it? You're jealous." She held up her hand to stop Pekin from responding. "You have nothing to be jealous about. *You're* Scout's girlfriend, not Vanessa."

"But what if——"

"What if what? I thought you were over that whole blaming Scout that Vanessa even exists thing. Scout didn't do anything wrong. In fact, to save your feelings, he declined to help her set up for the party."

Pekin crossed her arms and glowered at the floor before relaxing her arms with a sigh. "I know it's not *really* Scout's fault. But——"

"But nothing. It's not Scout's fault at all. This is because you don't value yourself. You think you don't measure up to her." Amber grabbed Pekin's shoulders and shook her. "Snap out of it! Sure, Vanessa is gorgeous, but so are you. Vanessa's smart, but so are you. And, not only are you smart and beautiful, you're kind and loyal and generous. And you're brave. How many ghosts has Vanessa faced down?"

Pekin looked up at Amber. "I know you're right."

"Of course I'm right, but I don't think you really believe it. So let me tell you this: Who knows you better than you? If you don't believe in yourself, who will? Scout and I love you. Scout didn't do a single thing wrong, and you're being massively unfair to hold a grudge against him over another girl. If you don't tell him you're not mad and that you want to go to Vanessa's party with him . . . well, just remember that he didn't want to talk to you for a week after you blamed him the first time. Are you ready for that to happen again? What more can he do to prove how much he cares for you? He saved your life twice!"

"He did, didn't he?" Pekin's expression eased from its tight frown, and a tiny smile appeared on her lips.

"Here's what I want you to do, Pekie," Amber said. "Stand up."

Pekin looked at her, head cocked questioningly, but she stood up facing her friend.

"Now," Amber continued, "throw your shoulders back and put your fists on your hips, legs apart."

Pekin giggled. "Like Wonder Woman?"

"Exactly like Wonder Woman. No one can stand like that and not feel like they can take on the world. When you walk in the door at Vanessa's party, you stand just like that for a minute, look around the room, and *know* that you're everything you need to be."

Pekin hugged Amber. "When did you get so smart?"

It was Amber's turn to blush. "I've always been smart."

"Yes, you have. And I love you too."

"So, are we good? Are you going to value yourself enough to go to Vanessa's party and hold your head high and not feel you're not good enough?"

"I'll try."

"That's not good enough. Believe me, and believe Scout. Both of us are telling you that you have nothing to worry about. So don't try. Promise me you're proud of yourself and you will not feel even a tiny bit jealous of Vanessa Dooley."

Pekin stood up and assumed a Wonder Woman stance. "I promise."

Then both girls collapsed on the bed in giggles.

CHAPTER TWENTY-FIVE

~~~~~~

MBER WAS ALREADY in the car when Scout picked Pekin up for their meeting with Matt. He was unusually quiet, as if he wasn't sure whether he was in the doghouse or not.

When Pekin climbed in the front seat, she caught Amber's glance warning her to be nice. Pekin had practiced her Wonder Woman stance several times that morning, and she couldn't help remembering the worry in Scout's eyes when he went home yesterday afternoon, so she pasted a warm smile on her face and leaned over to kiss him on the cheek, smiling even wider when he looked at her with a tentative question in his eyes.

"How are you guys this morning?" Pekin asked brightly, and Amber answered with a breezy "I'm good."

"Um, me too," Scout said.

"Well, I'm feeling great," Pekin said. "Looking forward to our meeting with Matt. I can't wait to see how he looks now that he's free of his mother's clutches."

"You might not see much difference," Scout said. "I mean, it's only been one day."

"Still, I can't wait."

I'm really not mad at Scout, Pekin was surprised to discover. She felt excited for the day.

THE FRONT DOOR TO THE antique shop was open when they arrived, and Matt hurried out to greet them with a huge grin.

"You look *great*," Pekin said with surprise. "I mean, after the last time we saw you."

"I feel so much better," Matt agreed.

"Have you noticed anything that might indicate your mother is still around?" Scout asked.

"No. It's so pleasant here now. Even the air seems fresher. Come in and see."

The kids followed him inside.

"I think I feel it too," Amber said, glancing around at the inside of the store. She took a deep breath. "Of course, you can't smell a ghost, but still . . ."

"I think it feels less *heavy*," Pekin said.

"I want to hear all about how you got her to leave," Matt said. "Oh, and here's the rest of what I owe you." He handed a folded check to Pekin.

She took a quick peek and stuffed it in the pocket of her shorts.

Matt hung his head. "I suppose I should feel bad that I didn't get to say goodbye to my mother before she crossed over."

"I think you saw enough of her to make up for missing

her final moments," Pekin said. "I don't think you should feel guilty about anything. You let her stay in spite of your misgivings."

"And if you'd been there," Amber said, "she might not have been willing to leave. I think she would have thought she still had a chance to win."

"They're right," Scout nodded. "You staying away was the right move. Try to remember the good things about your mom when you think about her. I'm sure she loved you, in her own way."

"Yeah, I suppose," Matt said. "She was a good mother while she was alive, and that's the way I'll think of her."

All of them leaned on their elbows on the counter as they discussed the events of the last few days.

"I feel a little bad about . . . all of it," Matt said when they were done. "It's too bad it didn't work out."

"It wasn't supposed to work out, really," Pekin said. "You gave her more than one chance to succeed in the arrangement, but she wanted more. She wanted to live your life. By stealing it from you."

"I think we got you away from her just in time," Scout said. "You were starting to look like a zombie."

"And you didn't seem to have control of your own mind," Amber added. "It was like Althea was calling the shots."

"Don't feel guilty about any of it," Pekin said. "You were a good and loving son. Now your mother is on the other side of the veil, where she should have been all along. When your time comes to cross over, you can meet her on equal ground. Maybe all the tension and betrayal will have evaporated and you can greet each other with open arms."

"That would be nice. And, you know what else is nice? Knowing that death isn't the end of everything. That there really is more to come."

"I hadn't thought about it like that," Pekin mused. "But you're right. It kind of takes some of the sting out of losing someone you love when you realize you can see them again."

After giving them a heartfelt thanks, Matt opened his arms for hugs all around, which came as a surprise, since Matt didn't seem like the huggy type.

The Ghosties waved goodbye to the happy client standing in the doorway of his shop and climbed into Scout's car.

"I feel really good," Pekin said with a contented sigh, leaning her head back against the front seat, eyes closed, big smile on her face.

"Me too," Amber said. "Are we done now?"

"I certainly hope so," Scout added.

"No more clients," Pekin said. "We'll enjoy the rest of summer break and then go back to being regular high school students again."

"I'm not sure we were ever *regular* high school students," Scout said.

Pekin punched his shoulder gently. "You know what I mean."

"I think I've forgotten how to be a normal kid," Amber said. "All that tension. And fear."

"What should we do now?" Scout asked. "We have the whole day before us with no ghosts in sight."

"Now," Pekin said wickedly, "we get ready for a party."

Scout looked at her in surprise. "Are you sure, Pekie?"

"I am absolutely sure. It'll be fun. Our first party together."

Amber reached up from the backseat and squeezed Pekin's shoulder. "Way to go, Wonder Woman."

CHAPTER TWENTY-SIX

PEKIN SHOULD HAVE FELT like sleeping in the day after wrapping up the Great Antique Store Caper. Oddly, she popped up earlier than she would have expected, feeling optimistic and energetic. She climbed out of bed after a quick snuggle with Griselda, then stretched as she watched her little cat hop off the bed and meow at the door to be let out.

"You're up early," her mother said when Pekin made an appearance in the kitchen in running shorts and sports bra. "Are you and Scout and Amber doing something this morning?"

"Not till later. It's such a gorgeous day. I'm going for a run to get a little exercise."

"I'll have some breakfast ready by the time you get back," her mom called to her daughter's back as Pekin slipped out the front door and pulled it closed behind her.

Pekin was half a block from her house when a scrawny dark calico cat darted out of the bushes and almost caused her to trip.

She stopped in her tracks, hands on hips and looked down at the cat, who stared boldly back.

Watch where you're going.

Pekin whipped around to see who had spoken, but the sidewalk was empty, and she turned back to the cat.

"Can you talk?" She cocked her head at the cat.

Can you hear me? the cat responded at the same moment.

Pekin's hand flew to her mouth, which had formed into a large "O."

She shivered, sure she couldn't have heard what she heard. She wasn't afraid, having already taken on four ghosts, but a talking cat was a whole different kind of weird. She leaned down, looking sharply at the cat, and straightened in surprise.

"Sparkle, is that you?"

Partially, the cat responded. *The rest is me*, continued a familiar voice.

"Mrs. Wagner?" It didn't seem possible. "But you died."

I know that, Pekin.

"So, why is your cat talking?"

My cat isn't talking. I am, the cat replied.

"But . . . but . . . but . . ." Pekin was having a hard time wrapping her head around what she was sure must be her imagination.

"But you *died*."

I'm aware of that, dear.

"And nobody could find Sparkle . . . I mean you . . . I mean Sparkle." She threw her hands in the air. "Oh, I don't know what I mean."

Of course they couldn't find her, Mrs. Wagner retorted. *I got her the heck out of Dodge.*

"But . . . why?"

There was no one to take her. She'd end up in the pound. You know what happens to them in the pound! The cat actually shuddered.

"I suppose," Pekin said doubtfully. "But you passed away more than a week ago. Who's been feeding Sparkle?"

Well, obviously, no one, the ghost responded. *We've had to forage . . . to dig through garbage.* Another cat cringe. *Sparkle's up there in years, so she's not as good a hunter as she once was. We've only had one bird in the last week. A sparrow. Can you imagine?*

"But why didn't you cross over like you were supposed to?"

I couldn't leave Sparkle alone to fend for herself. She's been my best friend for sixteen years. She has no one else; I couldn't just leave her. She would be devastated. And alone. I found her under a tree when she was only a couple of weeks old. I had to bottle feed her! I'm the only family she knows.

"That's thoughtful of you, I guess. I mean, keeping her company like that. Does she know you're in there?"

On some level. I can't tell what she's thinking. She has a cat brain after all. But she purrs a lot, and it's calm in here, so she's not afraid. I'm pretty sure she knows I'm here.

"How long are you staying?" Pekin asked, uncertain. "Isn't it crowded in there? Sparkle's still in there, too, right?"

Of course she is. But I doubt it will be much longer. Sparkle doesn't have a lot of time left.

"What happens when Sparkle, um, dies?" Pekin asked.

Then, my dear, we'll cross that rainbow bridge together.

Pekin couldn't help getting choked up, and she wiped a stray tear from her eye. "That's the sweetest thing I've ever heard," she said, bending down to pet the cat.

"May I?" She didn't want to forget her manners.

Of course you may, the cat said. *You can pick us up if you want.*

Pekin did. She snuggled her face into Sparkle's soft fur. "I'm taking you home and opening a can of cat food for you."

Can you make it two? The little cat looked at her with big round eyes. *We haven't had any real food in days.*

"Of course," Pekin answered.

Will your mother mind terribly?

"Not when I explain."

And she won't take us to the pound?

"Oh no. My mom wouldn't do that."

Sparkle relaxed in Pekin's arms, and the first real cat sound came out in the form of a purr.

Pekin turned back toward home, Sparkle and Mrs. Wagner resting blissfully in her arms.

She took a deep breath before opening the front door and facing her mother, prepared for the first moments of resistance she was sure she would face. But Melissa knew all about ghosts, and had had her own experiences with them when she was Pekin's age, so Pekin felt sure she would understand and be sympathetic to the situation.

Should we wait out here? the cat asked, looking up at Pekin with bright, round eyes.

"Maybe that would be a good idea," Pekin said, setting the cat down on the bench right inside the front door.

"Were you talking to someone?" Melissa asked when Pekin slid onto one of the island barstools and rested her elbows on the counter.

"Yes . . . no . . . I mean, maybe?"

Melissa turned from the sink where she'd been wiping crumbs off the counter. "Huh?"

"The thing is, Mom," Pekin said, gathering her courage. "I found Sparkle."

"Sparkle?" It took her mother a moment. "Mrs. Wagner's cat?"

"Uh-huh."

"I'm glad you found her. Poor thing must have escaped while people were coming and going from the house."

"She ran away."

"I'm sure she tried to get back inside. I wonder where she's been all this time."

"From the looks of her, she's had a hard time."

"We'll have to call someone—"

"No! We can't send her to the pound!" Pekin's face reflected her horror at the thought.

"Calm down, honey. I didn't say we'd send her to the pound. But we can't—"

"We have to keep her." Pekin crossed her arms over her chest and glared at her mother.

"Pekin, watch your tone. We don't need another cat. For one thing, Griselda would not be happy if you brought another cat into the house."

Sparkle wandered into the kitchen and sat, looking up at Melissa.

"Well, hello there," she said. "If looks could kill," she said over her shoulder to Pekin, "that cat is staring daggers at me. It's almost like she understood what I said."

Before Pekin could answer, Sparkle moved to stand with her paws on the refrigerator door.

"Oh, I forgot," Pekin said. "She's starving, so I have to get her something to eat." She hopped off the barstool and grabbed a can of cat food out of the cupboard and dumped the contents of the can onto a saucer. Sparkle immediately plunged her face into the plate, and loud purrs filled the kitchen.

"We need to talk about this," Melissa said. "We can't keep her."

The cat's head swung around, and she hissed at her.

"That's weird," Melissa said. "It's like she knows what we're talking about."

"She does, Mom," Pekin said. "Mrs. Wagner's in there with her. They're a package deal."

"Well, that's impos—" Melissa started, and looked at her daughter as it dawned on her what Pekin was telling her. "I don't understand."

"Mrs. Wagner moved in . . . so to speak . . . with Sparkle."

"But . . . why?"

Pekin slumped back onto the barstool. "She was afraid someone would take Sparkle to the pound, so she moved in, and the two of them ran away."

"So, Sparkle is a partially haunted cat."

"Yeah. That."

"But how long can she stay in there?"

"She said Sparkle is old and coming to the end of her life. Mrs. Wagner wants the two of them to cross over together."

"Aww, that's sweet."

"That's what I thought too. Mom, we can't give her to someone else who wouldn't understand."

Melissa squatted down, and Sparkle tentatively approached Melissa's outstretched hand. The cat nudged the hand with her head, and Melissa petted her thoughtfully. "Well, Mrs. Wagner, how nice to see you."

Sparkle immediately threw herself onto her back, offering her tummy for belly rubs, and purred loudly.

Thank you, the cat said.

Melissa's hand flew to her mouth, but a second later she regained her composure and said, "You're welcome."

"Mom, you can hear her too?"

She smiled. "I can!"

"So, you can see that we have to keep her, right?"

"Well, I—"

"Mom. No one else will get it. I'll take care of her . . . them. Griselda will get used to it . . . her . . . them. But we have to keep her." Pekin stared at her mother with naked pleading in her eyes.

Melissa sighed deeply. "Do you want to stay with us?" she asked the cat.

If you don't mind. We don't eat much. The cat rolled into a sitting position. *Except at first. We're starving.*

Melissa shook her head with an exasperated grin. "Well, then, welcome to the family."

Pekin gave an excited hop. "Thanks, Mom."

"Just remember, she's your responsibility."

Excuse me. I'm right here, the cat said.

"Oh," Melissa said, embarrassed. "Sorry, Mrs. Wagner. It's kind of hard to remember you and Sparkle are, uh, whatever you are."

You're still a human. I couldn't expect you to understand.

Melissa put her hands on her hips and glared at the cat. "I understand completely. It just takes some getting used to. And make sure you use the litter box."

The cat turned briskly and with a muffled *humph* stomped out of the kitchen. Pekin put a hand over her mouth to stifle the giggle that threatened to pop out at the sight of a cat stomping.

"Pekin—"

"I know, Mom. It's a period of adjustment for all three of us."

"Make that four. Your father will be sure to notice a new cat in the house."

"I suppose, but he likes Griselda, so I'm sure he'll be happy to have Sparkle live with us."

Melissa sighed. "He has mentioned that he wouldn't mind having another cat. So, I'm sure everything will be fine."

"Thanks, Mom. I guess I should go introduce her to Griselda," Pekin said, leaving the kitchen to find where Sparkle had wandered off to.

Pekin found the cat grooming herself at the foot of the stairs. She carried Sparkle up to her bedroom and locked her in. Then she went in search of Griselda, who was curled up on the sofa in the family room. She scooped her up and cuddled her as she carried the little cat up the stairs. She spent the short trip telling Griselda all about the new cat. Of course, Griselda didn't understand a word of it, and, when Pekin set her on the bed . . . the same bed where Sparkle was grooming herself . . . yowls and howls and growls burst forth from Pekin's little gray cat, who flew to the bedroom door, scratching frantically to get it to open so she could escape the intruder.

Pekin gathered Griselda up in her arms and tried to snuggle her, but Griselda was having none of it, wriggling and squirming to get out of Pekin's arms.

Instead of letting her go, Pekin sat on her bed, still holding her cat tightly, and freaked out when Sparkle hissed and spat at Griselda.

"That isn't helping!" Pekin said to Sparkle. "Mrs. Wagner! What are you doing?"

Don't forget, Pekin, Sparkle has her own opinion of what's going on. Cats aren't herd animals, you know.

"What has that got to do with anything? I'm not trying to form a herd here. I just want you and Griselda to try to get along. Can you do that?"

Well, ask Griselda. She started it.

"I don't speak cat, so I can't tell Griselda. As far as she's concerned, you're invading her space. What's your excuse?"

As I said, Sparkle has a mind of her own.

"Don't you have any influence over her? What am I saying? Of course you have influence over her. You made her run away. So get in there and tell her to be nice."

You were much more polite when I was alive, Pekin.

Pekin rolled her eyes up to the ceiling and said through gritted teeth, "Give me patience." Then she leveled her gaze on the new cat. "I'm sorry. I'll try to be nicer. Can we just start over?"

That's better, dear.

Griselda was squirming in Pekin's arms, trying to escape. Pekin ruffled her fur and scratched her head as she cooed to her, doing her best to reassure her little cat that the new one sitting on the bed wasn't a threat.

Sparkle began to purr and carefully approached Griselda, stopping a paw's length away. She reached forward with a paw and tentatively touched Griselda on the head. Griselda drew back, hissing.

The other cat actually seemed to shrug her shoulders. *I tried*, Mrs. Wagner said.

"Well, keep trying. If we have to sit here all night, you two are going to get along."

Keeping a tight hold on Griselda, Pekin reached into her back pocket for her phone with one hand and tapped Amber's number. A moment later, her best friend was on the phone.

"Hey, Pekie. What's up?"

"You won't believe what's going on here."

"Tell me, tell me!"

"You remember Mrs. Wagner, my neighbor who died last week?"

"Oh no! Don't tell me someone hired you to help her cross over into the light," Amber said, her voice rising.

"Not exactly. Kinda. Not really."

"Whaaat?"

"I'm sitting here in my room, holding Griselda while Mrs. Wagner's cat Sparkle is sitting on the bed too. Only Sparkle isn't only Sparkle. Mrs. Wagner moved in with her."

Silence on the other end.

"Sparkle's haunted!" Pekin announced.

"You have a cat ghost?"

"No. I have a cat sharing a body with a ghost. Mrs. Wagner's ghost."

"Uh-huh."

"And I'm keeping her, but Griselda doesn't like her and I don't know what to do."

"Does she not like her because Sparkle's a cat or because she's part ghost? Remember, Griselda never got used to Miranda."

"I don't know."

"Is it cold in your room? Because . . . you know."

"Hmm. Now that you mention it, when I was holding Sparkle, she seemed not quite body temperature. She was kind of like a little ice cube, but not as cold."

"Maybe that's what Griselda's picking up on. Anyway, good luck with that. I've gotta go to the market with my mom. I'll talk to you tomorrow to see what happened."

"Okay. Thanks, I guess."

"You don't need me to help you with the cats, do you?"

"Probably not. I'll figure something out. Bye."

"Looks like we're on our own," Pekin said to Sparkle and Griselda.

Chapter Twenty-Seven

~~~~~~

ONCE GRISELDA HAD ADOPTED an uneasy stillness, Pekin retrieved her journal and propped herself up against her headboard, intending to write down the events of the day. Pen poised, she suddenly laughed out loud.

What's so funny, dear? Mrs. Wagner asked, her whiskers twitching.

"It's just so ironic," Pekin responded. "The timing blows my mind." She gazed at the dark cat thoughtfully. "Scout and Amber and I can see ghosts—"

No, really? the cat said sarcastically. *I never would have guessed.*

"Don't be rude. I'm trying to explain it to you."

Sorry. Please proceed.

"Anyway, we just wrapped up our last case yesterday. The ghost was a mother who didn't want to cross over because she wanted to stay with her son so he wouldn't be alone."

That's so sweet! the cat purred. *I know just how she felt.*

"You'd think so. *We* thought so. At first. Until she turned evil." Pekin pulled down the top of her turtleneck so the cat could see her throat. "She tried to kill me."

The cat gasped. Which was a strange sound coming from a cat.

"It turned out that she didn't want to keep her son company. She wanted to absorb his energy so she could eventually take over his body and be alive again. Her son started looking pale and weak and . . . awful. I felt bad because he hired us to get rid of his ghost, and instead, we told him his mother was haunting his shop because she loved him too much to leave. We should have ignored her and just done our best to get her to cross over right away. But we fell for her story."

Pekin reached over and scratched Sparkle's head. "She didn't have a good heart like you do."

Thank you, dear.

"She ended up almost destroying her son."

What would have happened if she took over his body? Could she lead a normal life after that?

"Hmm, I don't know. But the ghost wasn't able to leave the antique shop she was haunting, so I'm not sure if, even if she managed to replace her son, she'd have been able to leave the shop. There's a lot about the world beyond that we don't know. Gosh, if we'd thought of that, it would have been a great argument to use on her. On the other hand, you could leave your house. Why could you?"

I don't know. I hadn't thought about it, but I never felt like I couldn't leave.

"Maybe it's because you moved in with Sparkle. Maybe

if you'd just stayed yourself, you would have been trapped in your house. I guess we'll never know."

I guess not. Did you get her to cross over?

"Yes, finally. We had to threaten to do a séance and call other entities to come out and drag her over to the other side. I appealed to her self-interest and told her how lonely she'd be because we were going to make sure her son never came back to the shop and she'd be all alone forever." Pekin giggled. "She was wearing a pink tracksuit and I told her I'd hate to go through eternity wearing a pink tracksuit. It kinda made her mad." She shook her head. "Anyway, after she thought about it, she grudgingly decided I was right and agreed to move on. Thank God! She was the *worst!*"

I'm not like that, the cat said. *I swear.*

"I believe you," Pekin said, and bent down to plant a kiss on Sparkle's head. "As I said, so ironic. Two mothers, two ghosts, two completely different intentions."

Griselda never took her eyes off the other cat and hissed periodically to make sure everyone knew where she was coming from.

Pekin wondered how bedtime would go. The bed belonged to Griselda, but she hated to make Sparkle sleep on the floor, where it wasn't as comfortable. But she also didn't want Griselda to feel insecure. Or replaced. Pekin left the two cats alone when she went down to dinner, and was concerned about what she'd find when she came back upstairs.

Her mother had already broken the news about the new

cat to Pekin's father by the time Pekin joined them at the dinner table. It was apparent that Melissa left out the part about the ghost of Mrs. Wagner being part of the deal.

He wasn't happy about another mouth to feed, even if it was a tiny mouth, but he wasn't immune to his daughter's argument that Sparkle had just lost her human and was elderly and didn't have a lot of time left, and how nice it would be to open their hearts and their home to the lonely cat.

By the time Pekin got back to her bedroom, there seemed to be an uneasy truce between the two cats. Pekin sat on the bed between them, a hand petting each of them. Sparkle was purring and, after a hesitation, Griselda purred too.

"What happened while I was gone?" Pekin asked Mrs. Wagner. "You and Griselda almost seem to be getting along."

I tried to appeal to her sympathy, acting all submissive. Apparently, she decided I wasn't as threatening as she'd initially thought. I wouldn't say we're friends now, but we touched noses.

"Oh, good. You don't have any idea what a relief that is."

For me, too. What if she never accepted me? Would you have had to send us away?

"I wouldn't have done that. We'd have worked something out. You and Sparkle are welcome here. I'm glad you're going to stay."

A round of texting before she turned out the light confirmed breakfast with Amber and Scout in the morning. Pekin couldn't wait to tell her best friends the latest. She thought a picture of the two cats together would be nice to share, so she held her phone up to snap one.

Hold on a moment, Sparkle said. *Let me just move a little closer.* The dark cat inched toward Griselda, who watched its approach warily. Careful not to get too close, Sparkle struck a pose . . . actually struck a pose! . . . and sat only inches away from Griselda. As Pekin held up her phone again, an extremely weird grin appeared on Sparkle's face just as she took the shot.

How did I come out? Mrs. Wagner, aka Sparkle, asked, standing at the edge of the bed so she could put a paw on Pekin's leg. *Show me! Show me!*

Pekin pulled up the photo, and her eyes widened. "What kind of look is that?" She turned the phone toward Sparkle so she could see.

I was smiling for the picture. I didn't want to appear glum.

"Let me just say, cats shouldn't smile. Those pointy canine teeth stick out."

I'm a cat. I don't have canine teeth. I have feline *teeth.* Sparkle flashed another cat smile at Pekin and began washing herself, sticking one of her hind legs into the air in a pork chop pose.

Pekin slid into bed and pulled the covers up to her neck, pleasantly surprised when Sparkle curled up on one side of her, and Griselda, after one last glare, curled up on the other side. Pekin sighed contentedly and closed her eyes.

Chapter Twenty-Eight

〰〰〰〰〰〰〰〰〰〰〰〰〰〰〰〰〰〰〰〰〰〰〰〰

B Y THE TIME SCOUT PULLED up at Pekin's to pick her up, Amber had filled him in on Pekin's new addition to the family.

For her part, Pekin was happy about the situation, so she didn't mind her friends' good-natured teasing.

"At least she doesn't want anything from us," Pekin said as she slid into the booth at Benny's. "We just have to let her stay with us for as long as Sparkle has left."

"Good, because there's no way she could pay our fee," Scout said, "unless she brought us a dead mouse or something."

"Mrs. Wagner said Sparkle's not a good hunter anymore. She's sixteen after all, so we don't have to worry about making change for a dead mouse."

"YOU GUYS WANT TO MEET Sparkle?" Pekin asked, leaning on her elbows on the grass at the edge of Lake Brawley. They'd made a beeline for the lake after breakfast, stopping at Scout's to pick up his cooler and at the market for turkey sandwiches and string cheese to take with them for lunch. "It's getting hot out here." She wadded up the sandwich wrapping and stuck out her hand for Scout's and Amber's, then carried their lunch trash over to one of the bins to recycle.

"Sure," Amber said. "I've never met a talking cat before."

"It's . . . an experience, all right," Pekin said. "And, bonus feature, she doesn't want anything from us." She brushed off the back of her shorts and started toward the car.

"I'm curious too," Scout said, as he and Amber stood to follow Pekin. "And I'm glad she's not an actual client. I've been thinking that it's been a rewarding experience having The Ghost Company and meeting interesting people and . . . other entities. But school's starting soon and football, and after that, college. I don't know how you guys feel about it, but maybe we should hang up our sage bundles. We solved three cases in one summer. I think that's a lot. What do you guys think?"

Pekin's face fell, and she looked down and began minutely examining her cuticles.

"I'm sorry, Pekie," Scout said quickly. "I mean, we don't have to make a decision right now, and if something else comes up, we can see if we have time to do it."

"That's not it, Scout," she replied. "I know what you're saying, and you're right. It's just, well, I felt so important. No, that's not what I mean. I felt like we made a difference, to people and to the ghosts we managed to release into the light. And I guess I'm a little disappointed to be going back to being just a high school girl."

"You're never *just* anything, Pekie," he said, putting a comforting arm around her shoulders and pulling her close. "You're The Amazing Pekin Dewlap, and I lo—" He cleared his throat. "And I love you."

She couldn't stop the little tear that slipped down her cheek, or the huge smile that broke out. "I love you, too, Scoutie."

"Um," Amber cut in. "I'm still here." At the embarrassed looks on her friends' faces, Amber laughed. "I'm just kidding, you guys. It's about time!"

Pekin grabbed Amber in a bear hug. "We love you, too, Amber."

AMBER AND SCOUT SAT ON Pekin's bed staring at the dark cat, who stared right back at them.

"Hi, Sparkle," Amber said, reaching out a tentative hand for the cat to sniff before she nudged her, giving Amber permission to scratch her head.

Sparkle stepped across Amber's lap to inspect Scout up close. He hesitated a moment, then ran his hand down Sparkle's back and ruffled her fur. Sparkle immediately rolled onto her back for belly rubs.

Scout scratched her tummy for a few moments.

"Cute, isn't she?" Pekin said.

Don't stop, Sparkle said when Scout removed his hand, and both Amber's and Scout's eyes grew big.

"Um, okay?" Scout said and resumed scratching the cat's tummy.

When she was satisfied, the cat rolled over again. *That's enough for now.*

Amber noticed Griselda sitting in a corner, glaring at the newcomer. She got off the bed and approached the little gray cat. "Aw, do you feel left out?" She picked Griselda up and carried her back to the bed to cuddle.

Griselda's gaze didn't leave Sparkle, and she hissed to make sure everyone knew her position on the subject of adding a new cat to the family.

"Don't be mean, Griselda," Amber said, holding Griselda up and kissing the top of her head. "Sparkle's a sweet cat. You should be friends with her."

Fat chance, Sparkle said. *We've gone out of our way to be nice to her, but you can see how she returns the favor.*

"Give her time," Amber said. "It's a big change to her life."

Scout crossed his arms and watched the exchange.

We'll get along. It's not like we'll be staying forever.

"I hope you'll be here for a long time, though," Pekin said.

We'll see, Sparkle said. *We're doing much better after having regular meals.*

"Personally, I'm glad about that," Pekin said, picking up the scrawny dark cat in a hug. "I hope your stay won't be a short one."

Thanks, but Sparkle doesn't like that, Mrs. Wagner said as the cat struggled to release itself from Pekin's embrace. *You're squeezing us.*

"Oh, sorry," Pekin said. "I didn't realize."

You could introduce us to your friends, Mrs. Wagner, aka Sparkle, said.

"That's right," Pekin responded. "They've never met you." She pointed to Amber and Scout in turn and made the introductions.

Isn't it time for a snack? the cat asked as it hopped off the bed and sauntered to the bedroom door. *We're still very thin, you know.*

Pekin sighed. "I suppose it wouldn't hurt. I'm sure you'll be able to eat again when it's dinnertime." Looking at Amber, who still held Griselda, Pekin said, "You should bring Griselda. I'm sure she'd like a snack too."

CHAPTER TWENTY-NINE

TWO DAYS LATER, SCOUT invited Pekin and Amber to go to Lake Brawley again.

"I have something to show you. I want it to be a surprise, so can you have one of your parents give you a ride?"

"That's so mysterious!" Pekin said. "I'll see if my mom can take us."

She and Amber giggled excitedly on the trip out to the lake and thanked Pekin's mother for the ride.

The girls tromped toward Scout, who sat on a blanket in the spot where they usually hung out, his back to them.

"So, what's the surprise?" Amber asked as they approached, and he turned around, flashing a huge grin and cradling a wiggling puppy in his arms.

"Scout! You didn't!" Pekin's eyes widened, and she smiled.

"A dog?" Amber shrieked. "You got a dog!" She clapped her hands and bounced up and down.

He laughed. "Almost. It's the family's dog. My little sister Kerrie conned my mom into letting her take one of the puppies she found at the mall yesterday. The pet store was having an adoption event. Kerrie barely allowed me to borrow it . . . *him* to show you. His name is Kombucha, after her current favorite health fad."

"Kombucha!" Amber gushed. "I love it. Can I hold him?"

The puppy squirmed in her arms, and Pekin scooted close to Amber so she could pet Kombucha, too. He was a gray-black terrier mix of some kind, with scruffy hair and one ear that flopped over and one that stood up straight, and he probably weighed only five pounds. Tiny and adorable.

"I want to hold Buchie next," she said, beaming at Scout. "We knew you'd end up with a dog. You fell in love with the Dwyers' dog, Spike."

"Kerrie won't allow you to call him Buchie," Scout said. "Just so you know."

Amber deposited Kombucha in Pekin's lap. "We wanted you to name your new dog Sparky."

"Yeah. I suggested that name to Kerrie, but she wouldn't go for it. She found him and thought it was only fair that she got to name him."

"Does he talk?" Pekin cocked her head and narrowed her eyes at Scout.

And he laughed. "No, he does not talk. No ghost is sharing space in this puppy."

"That's a relief, I guess," she said. "Although, I like having a talking cat."

Scout took the puppy back and set him down, tossing a

ball, which Kombucha immediately dashed after. In an instant, all three kids were on their feet racing around after the frisky pup, who couldn't help tripping over his feet as he romped in the grass by the lake.

Chapter Thirty

PEKIN SETTLED ONTO HER BED with her journal and began jotting her thoughts down in the diary. She had tons to write about Scout's new puppy. He hadn't wanted to get a dog since he'd be going off to college in a year and would be busy during his senior year of high school with football and schoolwork. But that didn't mean he wouldn't love having a dog in the house. Thank you, Kerrie.

If I hear "Evergreen" one more time, I think my ears will explode, she wrote, changing topics. *Amber came over this afternoon so I could help her practice the song. It's for her grandparents' fiftieth wedding anniversary tonight, and she and her cousins are going to wear matching dresses and perform the song. Amber's so nervous. She shouldn't be. Her voice is great. And Josh will be there for moral support. I guess I'll hear all about it tomorrow. And there'll probably be video.*

Griselda, who was curled in a ball by Pekin's knee, raised her head and hissed as Sparkle jumped onto the bed. Pekin only had two hands, and, luckily, there were only two cats, so she could pet them simultaneously, lulling them into peaceful purrs.

She drew her knees up and rested her chin on them in thought, studying Sparkle.

"What's it like?" Pekin asked Mrs. Wagner, who tilted her head to look up at Pekin.

What's what like, dear?

Pekin cleared her throat. "You know, dying."

But you've dealt with several ghosts, dear. Didn't they tell you?

"No, not really. It was never the right situation. Our first ghost, Miranda, had been murdered a century ago. She wouldn't have been the right one to ask, as it wasn't a natural death. Our second ghost, Lily, died in childbirth and was only focused on finding her lost child. And our last ghost, Althea, wasn't interested in that kind of a conversation. She was too self-absorbed. I was just curious, that's all. You don't have to answer if you don't want to."

I don't mind. I passed in my sleep, so it was peaceful. One moment I was in my body, and the next I was floating up near the ceiling. I could see Sparkle patting my face with her paw, and I could feel her concern. She knew I was gone, but she curled up by my side, only looking up now and then to see if I'd come back. At some point, there were others in the room. My daughters and people I didn't recognize. I watched as my daughters discussed Sparkle. Neither wanted to take her home with them and felt a shelter was the best solution. That's when I knew I had to rescue Sparkle, who was huddled under the dresser, peering out in fear, not knowing what to do.

I floated down so I could see her eye to eye, and she saw me. She was frightened and scooted back until she hit the wall, but I talked to her soothingly and she relaxed and started to purr. I didn't plan to jump into her. It just happened when the idea came to me. I found myself in a warm space and realized we were in there together. She didn't seem to mind. In fact, she was peaceful about it. I wasn't, though. I knew I had to get her to safety somehow, and we quietly made our way to the front door, slinking around the edges of each room, waiting for an opportunity to escape. When the . . . I hate to say it . . . morgue attendants were coming in and out of the house, no one noticed when Sparkle and I slipped out the door.

Sparkle had mostly been an indoor cat, so I took over the job of figuring out where to go. Of course, I hadn't ever foraged for food, so we had to figure that out together. She remembered how to catch birds from when she was young . . . I let her go outside sometimes back then . . . but she lost a step or two as she got old, so there was just that one sparrow. Can't say I loved it. All those feathers.

I didn't have to convince her to stay in the shadows, since that's a natural cat trait. We tried to keep out of sight of humans as much as possible. And then, like a miracle, you appeared. End of story.

"Thanks for comparing me to a miracle," Pekin laughed. "But, really, I'm relieved I found you and could help you out. It's nice having you around."

It's nice to be *around. Sparkle is such a sweet cat. I know you'll take good care of her. Of us.*

"Well, it's almost bedtime," Pekin said, closing her journal and returning it to the drawer in her nightstand.

Do you think you could get us a snack? Sparkle asked, blinking wide, trying for puppy dog eyes. Which wasn't very effective since cats don't have puppy dog eyes.

Chapter Thirty-One

~~~~~~

THE SATURDAY NIGHT OF Vanessa Dooley's party had finally arrived. Walking in the door of the gymnasium, Scout had a tight grip on Pekin's hand. She fought down the butterflies in her stomach, determined to feel only good emotions.

The gym was already swarming with kids sitting on bleachers and standing in clumps, walking around carrying red Solo cups. They looked like they were having fun, talking and dancing and gathering around the DJ spinning discs at the back of the gymnasium.

Vanessa Dooley waved from across the gym and swept up to greet the four teens as soon as she spotted them, leaning in to give Scout a hug, then, almost as an afterthought, giving Pekin a hug as well. Although it was maybe a little more stiff-armed than the one she'd given Scout.

"I'm so glad you all came," Vanessa gushed, her eyes on Scout.

Amber glanced at Pekin to see how she was dealing with being in Vanessa's orbit.

"I'm glad to be here," Pekin said, dragging Vanessa's

attention away from Scout. "The gym looks wonderful! You did a great job."

Vanessa looked Pekin up and down and glanced at Scout, as if she was curious why he was with Pekin. She seemed to shrug. "It was a lot of work but worth it." She shot a coy glance at Scout. "Even if you bailed on helping me get the gym ready for my party."

"I'm sorry Scout and I weren't able to help you," Pekin said, pulling Vanessa's attention back to her. "It's been a busy summer for us."

Josh bumped Amber's shoulder. "Your mouth is open," he said under his breath.

Amber blushed, turning so that she was facing away from her friends, and said, also under her breath, "Oh, sorry. I'm just so freaked out about how well Pekin's doing. She's actually talking to Vanessa!"

"Why would that freak you out?"

"You don't know the history of Pekin and Vanessa Dooley."

"There's history?"

"Not exactly history. Vanessa probably hardly knows who Pekin is, but Pekin has . . . had . . . an inferiority complex about Vanessa. Because of Scout. She thought Vanessa liked Scout."

"But Scout's Pekin's boyfriend, right?"

"Right, but . . . it's a girl thing. We worry sometimes about being enough."

"Enough of what?"

"Oh, Josh! It's too complicated to explain. Let's just go get something to drink."

Amber grabbed Josh's arm and led him toward the refreshments table. She looked over her shoulder, and Pekin smiled at her and waved her hand in an *I'm okay* gesture.

"Why?" Vanessa Dooley asked pointedly. "What were you doing that had you so busy?"

"We had a summer job," Scout said, slipping an arm around Pekin's shoulders. "I think we're done for now, though. Time to have some fun."

"Oh yeah. I remember. You guys were playing at being ghostbusters." Her face reflected her condescension.

"We weren't playing, actually," Scout said. "But no big deal."

"Great DJ," Pekin said, beaming at Vanessa. "Scout and I have to go dance."

Once on the dance floor, Pekin couldn't help glancing back at Vanessa, who did *not* have a smile on her face.

"You okay?" Scout asked, looking down at her.

"Couldn't be better. I'm so glad we came tonight."

Scout picked her up in his arms and twirled her around happily, before setting her back down. "Thanks."

"You're welcome," she replied.

Amber and Josh soon joined them, dancing carefully so their drinks wouldn't slosh out of the red plastic cups, giggling when they did.

The music was blaring, and the gym floor was packed with rowdy kids. An hour later, Vanessa Dooley approached Scout and Pekin, who were trying to catch their breath after nonstop dancing. She barely acknowledged Pekin as she put a hand on Scout's arm and asked him to dance with her, smiling up into his eyes.

Scout glanced at Pekin and patted Vanessa's hand as he picked it up and removed it. "Sorry, Vanessa. All my attention is for my girlfriend tonight."

Vanessa was gracious about the rejection, which couldn't have been easy since a trio of her friends was watching from the sidelines. Pekin couldn't help but notice the way Vanessa narrowed her eyes as she tried not to stomp off the dance floor.

Pekin felt Scout's gaze and looked up at him. His face was open and hopeful.

Her heart was brimming that he'd told Vanessa that Pekin was his girlfriend, and she raised up on her tiptoes and kissed him, earning a bear hug.

Later, when Pekin and Amber visited the girls' bathroom, Pekin said, "Should I have been generous and told Scout he could dance with Vanessa?"

"Nah," they said at the same time, then burst out laughing.

"Nice thought, though," Amber said, bumping Pekin's shoulder with her own as they walked back to the dance floor.

The party Pekin had dreaded turned out to be more fun than she could have hoped for. They all danced until their feet almost fell off. The best part was when Scout introduced her to the football players on his team. She and Scout hadn't been together when the school year ended, so none of them except for Josh knew about her. Scout was popular with the other players, and they made a big deal out of meeting Pekin.

This might have been the happiest she'd ever been. And she glowed whenever she looked at Scout, thinking she'd never forget this night.

Pekin had an eleven o'clock curfew, so by ten-thirty the kids were saying their goodbyes. Pekin noticed that Vanessa's glare followed them out the door of the gym.

Walking through the parking lot to Scout's car with her friends, Pekin felt calm and happy, proud of herself that she'd managed to be in the same room with Vanessa and not melt into a puddle of anxiety. She sighed contentedly and leaned her head on Scout's shoulder, snuggling under the arm he had around her shoulders.

Even at ten-thirty it was warm and pleasant, and nothing could mar the bubble of joy she found herself in.

And then it wasn't warm and pleasant. A distinct chill filled the air, and Pekin pulled away from Scout and glanced around. "Are you guys cold?" she asked, shivering.

"Yes!" Amber said, hugging herself, her eyes big.

"What—" Scout started, stopping abruptly when a gray blur floated into their path.

"What's that?" Amber whispered in alarm.

As they watched, the blur shimmered, and a human form took shape.

Help me.

"What's going on?" Josh asked, gawking at his friends.

Pekin sighed. "Not something we were hoping to see. Maybe our end-of-summer fun is going to have to wait awhile longer."

Smiling wryly at Scout and Amber, she said, "Sorry, you guys. Looks like we'll be doing this one for free."

ACKNOWLEDGMENTS

I have to thank my usual suspects. They know who they are.

But, for those who don't know, my usual suspects include my sisters Sheila Baldwin and Michelle Hutton, who are always ready to read and comment on multiple drafts of my stories, and Elise and Maya Crocker, who are quick to offer suggestions and ideas. And many other supportive friends and family who keep my spirits up, so to speak.

My thanks also to my wonderful editor, Shelly Stinchcomb, and guest editors Lindsey Carter and Michael Cagle, whose attention to detail upped my game; Debra Kennedy, who formatted my novels; Dane at eBook Launch for the incredible cover art, Acorn Publishing, and the Acorn team, Jessica Therrien and Holly Kammier, all of whom helped pave my path to publication.

As always, thanks to everyone who leaves me a review. Those reviews on Amazon, Goodreads, and other spots just might tempt someone to read my books! And, who knows? With enough reviews, I just might make Amazon's best-seller list!

IF YOU HAVEN'T READ THE FIRST BOOK IN THE SERIES YET,
AND WANT TO SEE WHERE IT ALL BEGAN,
BE SURE TO CHECK OUT
THE HAUNTING OF ELMWOOD MANOR
A PEKIN DEWLAP MYSTERY

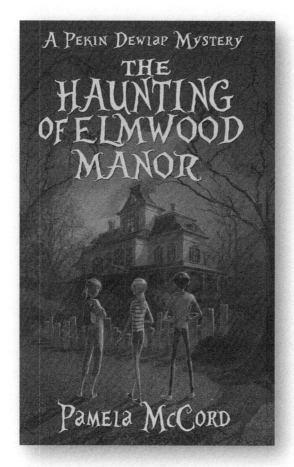

Available on:

- **Amazon**
- **Barnes and Noble**
- **most other major online retailers**

Made in the USA
Monee, IL
04 March 2024

54396092R00142